diary of a 6th grade ninja 4

a game of chase

BY MARCUS EMERSON
AND NOAH CHILD

ILLUSTRATED BY DAVID LEE

EMERSON PUBLISHING HOUSE

This one's for Evelyn...

Text copyright © 2013 by Emerson Publishing House.
Illustrations copyright © David Lee

Emerson Publishing House

Book design by Marcus Emerson.

Chase Cooper here, and if you know who I am, then you'll know my first few months at Buchanan School were some of the craziest months of my life. Ninja clans, pirates, food drives, skating parties, and stolen love notes are just a little taste of what's happened to me at this school.

But if you were to tell me things were only going to get *crazier* as my sixth grade year went on, then I would've muttered something sarcastic at you while shaking my fist.

I'm a sixth grader at Buchanan School, which is unlike any other school I've ever heard of. What exactly do I mean? Well, the last school I went to didn't have secret ninja clans or pirate meetings. Some say it has something to do with the building being named after James Buchanan, but I don't know enough about presidents to argue with that. All I know is Buchanan was the fifteenth president, and the only one who *didn't* have a wife. A president's wife is normally the First Lady, but since he didn't have a wife, it was his *niece* that was the First Lady. Weird, right?

At the start of the school year, I was the new kid, but I can't use that excuse much longer since this is my *fourth* month here. Sure, I'm still getting to know everyone in the school, but I wouldn't say I was "fresh meat" anymore.

On the second day of school, I was recruited into a ninja clan by a kid who turned out to be just another bully in a sea of bullies. I was given the leadership position of the ninja clan soon after that due to the fact that their old leader was a jerk.

My appearance hasn't changed much, except for the obvious fact that we're all growing older no matter how hard we try not to. I'm probably an inch or two taller, which would be awesome if the rest of my body were filling out too, but it's not. I actually look like I'm getting *skinnier*. No big deal though. I've learned to roll with the punches.

Am I still the shy guy I was at the beginning of the year? You bet – that's not something that can change overnight, but I think I'm getting better in that area too.

If you read my last diary, you'll remember that I totally *owned* Wyatt and Carlyle on the skate floor; beating Carlyle in a race, and schooling Wyatt in a game of Shoot the Duck. Speeches were made, soda was had, and friendships grew stronger.

…except for one friendship.

Brayden is still holding a grudge against me for not speaking up when I should have. The school paper posted a picture of a ninja running from the monitors, and then

Brayden was caught investigating the crime in *his* ninja outfit. Everyone assumed he was the ninja in the picture. I know he was only trying to help, but he goofed up and got a day in detention for it. He *shouldn't* have done it, but I know I probably could've done *something* to prevent it. At least I think I could've. We've barely said a word to each other in the last month, which bums me out, but it's not like *I'm* the one who did anything wrong. He'll come around. I just hope it's before we graduate.

Faith is as cool as ever. We're still science lab partners, and I've gotten to know her better over the past month. She's *way* more into video games and horror movies than I originally thought, which takes her to *epic* levels of awesome. It turns out one of her hobbies is watching awful movies while making fun of them the entire time – just like Brayden and I *used* to do.

My cousin Zoe has been pretty busy too. I haven't seen her much after school or for Sunday brunch between our families because she got the lead role in a play coming up in about a month. I think the play is about an orphaned girl that's adopted by a rich dude – odd, if you asked me, but I guess the play is a classic from like, a hundred years ago.

The more I talk to Gavin, the hall monitor captain, the more I like the kid. He's from Texas, which explains why he sounds like such a cowboy. He's one of the few in this school who knows my secret – that I'm the leader of a secret ninja clan that trains in the shadows. He's cool though so I trust him with that knowledge.

He also helped Zoe and I escape the red ninjas a month ago. While my cousin and I were investigating the spot I thought they trained in, three of those guys cornered us. After getting chased through a few empty rooms, Gavin pulled us aside and kept us hidden. Did he save our lives that day? Probably. Did he yank on my arm hard enough to bruise me? Not gonna say. Did Zoe develop a super crush on him because he rescued her? Yes, and gross.

Which brings me to Wyatt and the red ninja clan. I know they're here at the school, and I know exactly which students are in the clan because they all wear a red band around their wrists. Apparently everyone who joins Wyatt's clan gets one of those "friendship bracelets" so they know who else is a red ninja. I wonder if they get a *sticker* too.

Surprisingly, Wyatt hasn't messed with me since the skating party. He still shoots an angry look my way when I pass him in the hallway, but other than that, *nothing*. On the one hand, it's been nice, but on the other hand, it's kind of freakin' me out like he's planning something. And on yet another hand maybe he's learned his lesson. And then again on that hand over there, maybe he's given up! That's like, *four* hands!

The red ninjas have kept a low profile as well. It's weird because there was a ton of activity that first week I discovered them, but not a lot since then. I can't say I'm sad about it. In fact, I'm just the opposite. Zoe thinks that as long as they stay hidden and away from me, I'm better off pretending they don't even exist. I'm inclined to agree with her opinion on the matter. Maybe it has something to do with the whole *"ignore them and they'll leave you alone"* thing.

But at Buchanan School, there's more going on behind the scenes than anyone realizes, and this month things took a turn for the strange. It happened right after I got to school on Monday morning… funny how evil likes to get a fresh start on Mondays. Now I know why most adults *hate* that day…

"Well well well," said a raspy voice from behind me. "If it isn't the *hero* of Buchanan himself!"

My stomach dropped as I turned around, afraid that Wyatt had finally snapped. To my delightful surprise, it wasn't him. "Zoe!" I gasped at a high enough pitch that my throat hurt. "That wasn't even a little funny! You sounded like a *dude*!"

She smirked. "Normally I'd sock you for saying something so rude, but I'll let it go this time since your voice squeaked like a little girl."

I chuckled as I swung my nasty locker open. The number on the silver plate at the top was crusted over and hanging by a single nail, hammered directly above the number 108.

"Lucky one-oh-eight," I whispered as metal clanged against metal, revealing the terrible mess of papers inside.

I actually felt proud that my locker looked the way it did. It's one of those messes that's *so bad* that nothing moves. Everything was packed into it so tightly that my stuff never fell out. All my textbooks were on the top shelf, but every single assignment, book report, and any other loose-leaf sheet of paper had been mashed into the bottom of the locker. The pile was about a foot and a half high already – I was hoping to fill the entire five feet of locker space by the end of the year. If you're gonna go, go all out, right?

"OMG," Zoe whispered as she gazed at my glorious paper stack. "Your mother would cry if she saw this."

I laughed. "I think at my age, it'd take a lot more than a dirty locker to make her cry. And the papers aren't even the *worst* of it. I'm pretty sure there are half eaten sandwiches somewhere near the bottom."

Zoe cupped her hands over her mouth. "Serious?"

I smiled proudly.

My cousin turned her back and started heading for homeroom. She held her hand up and whipped it backward. "Boys are so *gross*."

"See you in class!" I hollered as I turned back to my locker. Grabbing the books off the top shelf, I pushed them into my book bag. Ever since I decided not to store my ninja outfit in my bag, I've had more than enough room for my school supplies, which I *guess* should come first.

During the second and third month of school, my ninja robes had fallen out of my hands. When Carlyle was threatening to take down my cousin Zoe, I gave them to him in exchange for leaving her alone. And just last month, my outfit was stolen by Wyatt and then used to commit a string of crimes at Buchanan.

I now wear my ninja outfit *under* my street clothes. There's no way I'm giving them up again! It sounds like it would get hot, but it's actually pretty cozy since the weather is growing colder. I also switched my top to one with a hood. If we were to run into each other at a ninja convention, you'd probably say something like, "My word, what *handsome* ninja robes you're wearing!"

And for those of you wondering – yes, Buchanan is *still* searching for the ninja featured in the school paper. The few kids who know I'm the leader of a ninja clan know it *wasn't* me, but it's probably not enough to convince the rest of the school.

Because of that picture, the school president gave the order to demolish the wooded area by the track and field on the anonymous tip that ninjas trained there. You and I *both* know who it probably was that gave the tip.

The hallway became quiet as I zipped up my bag, which was a bad sign. It meant the bell was going to ring at any second. Hoisting the bag over my shoulders, I took one last glance into my locker to see if I was forgetting anything. It was at that moment when something caught my eye – a small black object resting right on top of my trash pile. I don't know how I had missed it before.

"What are *you?*" I whispered, picking up the object between my two fingers. As I brought it closer to my face, I realized it was a black chess piece, the little horse to be exact. I think it was called a knight.

It definitely wasn't *my* chess piece because I find the game boring. I'm not too familiar with it, only having played it a couple times on my dad's cell phone, but it just wasn't for me. I'm more of a "*shoot the alien zombies*" kind of gamer.

Then I noticed a yellow sticky note sitting under the piece. Right away I could see there was handwriting on it, which at this point in my life, made my stomach turn.

Every note I had received at this school was always bad news so it was likely that this wasn't going to be good. I picked it up and read it.

Chase,
I know your secret. The game has begun. Play along or I'll tell the entire school what you are.
- Jovial Noise

Jovial Noise? Was *Jovial* their name? Did a psycho super villain leave this for me? Great. Seriously, what's with kids leaving creepy notes for me? It almost felt like Buchanan School had it out for me.

Raising my fist, I shook it mightily. "James Buchanan!" I groaned, hoping the fifteenth president was rolling in his grave.

I folded the sticky note in half and slipped it into my pocket. How did these things get into my locker in the first place? I looked up at the slits near the top of the metal door, but the chess piece was too fat to have fit through any of those. Someone had to have *opened* my locker to get it in there…

…but *who* would do that?

The bell to homeroom started ringing. When I turned around, I saw I was the only kid left in the hallway. "Great," I muttered as I started jogging to class. "Late *again!*"

Monday. 7:47 AM. Homeroom.

Mrs. Robinson was already at the front of the room making the morning announcements when I finally made it to homeroom. Luckily none of the hall monitors caught me or I would've been busted for sure. Slipping into the room, I took my usual spot behind Zoe. Mrs. Robinson made saw me walk in late, but winked. I didn't think she'd care.

"Nice," Zoe whispered. "You've decided to stop cutting it close and just be tardy, huh?"

I nodded. "You know me. Being on time is for the *birds*," I replied. I never understood what that meant, but if I use the phrase enough, maybe I'll get it one day.

Mrs. Robinson leaned against the dry erase board and casually gave the announcements. "As many of you already know there's going to be some mild construction in the cafeteria in the next couple of weeks. After an unfortunate accident involving the kitchen and some burnt toast, we've discovered that our sprinkler system is outdated and needs to be replaced."

"An unfortunate accident?" a student up front asked. "You mean when the sprinklers automatically switched on when they shouldn't have?"

Mrs. Robinson folded her hands. "*That's* actually the problem. Our sprinklers are so old that they need to be *manually* switched on by a crank in the cafeteria."

"It's *not* automatic?" the student barked. "Geez, is it from the dark ages? Are there a bunch of rats somewhere in the school that run on treadmills to make the thing work?"

The rest of the students laughed, but not me. I was too busy imagining how *awesome* rat fire fighters would've been, all drivin' around in their tiny rat fire trucks.

Another student from the side of the room raised her hand, but spoke before being called on. "I'm in the cafeteria all the time," she said, raising her voice at the end of the sentence so it sounded like a question. "How come I haven't seen any kind of switch like that before?"

Mrs. Robinson rolled her eyes. "I'm probably saying too much, but the switch is behind a locked door. No one's gettin' in there without a key."

My classmates nodded in unison. There were a lot of "of course," and "go figure," sounds coming from different parts of the room.

"But seriously," Mrs. Robinson murmured. "We'll

be upgrading all that stuff so the cafeteria will be a little busier than normal. Lunch times won't change at all."

A couple students sighed in relief. I guess some kids *really* like school lunch.

Mrs. Robinson continued. "Of course you *also* know that the new Buchanan sign will be coming at the end of the week, but the new jerseys for P.E. should be here today or tomorrow so if you placed an order, I think Coach Cooper will have them waiting for you at the beginning of your P.E. class."

I always thought it was weird to call gym class P.E. or even worse, *physical education* or *phys ed* for those who only have enough time to say half the words. All that sounded so cold and cruel. Why not just call it "gym?"

"The new jerseys will have our new mascot," Mrs. Robinson sighed. "That our very own *Chase Cooper* spent over a month choosing."

The other kids in class turned in their seats, gawking at me. I folded my arms and slouched a little, trying to hide from their disappointed eyes.

Since I beat Carlyle a couple months ago on the Norwegian obstacle course, I was given the opportunity to choose a new mascot for the school.

I took a long time deciding what our new mascot would be because I wanted it to be something awesome that'd strike *fear* into the hearts of other schools! But then I thought, wait a second… did we want to strike *fear* into them? Or win games? If we were something cool like the "Panthers," then we wouldn't stand out from other schools so I decided on a mascot that seemed harmless. Something that we could all stand behind as a student body. Something *majestic* and *proud*. Something to make other schools think we *weren't* as awesome as we were. You see, I wanted to choose a mascot that would mess with their heads just enough so that they wouldn't play as hard. Buchanan's victory would be swift and unexpected!

We *used* to be called the Buchanan *Wildcats*.

Now we're called the Buchanan *Moose*.

Mrs. Robinson proceeded to talk to the class. Everyone returned their attention to her, but Zoe kept herself turned toward me.

My cousin tightened her lips and frowned as she stared into my soul. "*What* were you thinking?"

"I don't know!" I said defensively. "I guess I thought we'd have an advantage because other schools wouldn't take us seriously!"

"But a *moose*?" Zoe asked, clearly disgusted.

"It sounded like a good idea at the time!" I replied.

Zoe shook her head with a smile. As upset as she might've been, I knew she found it a *little* funny. Finally, she said, "The weirdest part is that it sounds like you're talking about a *single* moose. *One* moose. A *moose* at Buchanan. The Buchanan moose."

"I know!" I said. "But '*moose*' is plural for moose! Trust me! I *tried* to get Principal Davis to agree with calling us the Buchanan *Meese*, but he refused!"

"That's because *meese* isn't a word!" Zoe said.

I leaned back in my seat. "False," I said bluntly.

"The plural for goose is *geese* so it only makes sense that the plural for moose is *meese*."

I could see Zoe's jaw drop slowly, but I kept talking.

"It just makes so much sense to say *meese!*" I insisted. "We could say, 'there goes a flock of geese!' So then we could also say, 'there goes a flock of meese!'"

Zoe swallowed hard. "My goodness, for the first time in my life, I can actually *feel* myself getting dumber from our conversations! A *flock* is a term only used for *birds!"*

I shrugged my shoulders. "Sorry," I said sarcastically. "Then I guess it would be a *herd* of meese."

"*Meese isn't a word!*" Zoe shouted angrily.

Mrs. Robinson stopped her announcements as the class turned toward us again.

"Is everything alright back there?" Mrs. Robinson asked, concerned.

Blushing, Zoe spun in her chair to face the front of the room. "Yes, sorry."

The homeroom teacher paused for a moment, staring at my cousin and I. Shrinking in her chair, Zoe mumbled another apology before Mrs. Robinson spoke again. Once the teacher was back into her speaking groove, I leaned forward in my desk.

Pulling the small chess piece from my bag, I tapped it on my cousin's shoulder. "Look what I found in my locker this morning."

Zoe didn't turn around. "I don't care."

"C'mon," I whispered as I held it in front of her face. "Look! This little horse thing was sitting on my pile of papers."

Zoe didn't turn her head enough for me to see her face, but I knew she was looking at the chess piece. "So what? It's a knight," she said.

"But someone got into my locker and put it there," I said. "What do you think it could mean?"

"I think it means your locker has come to life and wants to play you in a game of chess," she said sarcastically. "Maybe the school's out to get ya."

I chuckled quietly. "Funny 'cause I had the same thought. I'd probably *still* lose if that happened. What if it's like, a sign or something? Maybe this is somebody's way of telling me I'm their knight in shining armor?"

Zoe snorted. A few of the kids around us turned to look as she contained her laughter. "A knight in shining armor – good one."

"Whatever," I sighed, leaning back in my seat. "It's possible. Maybe it's from a girl too shy to speak to me herself so she—"

Zoe interrupted me. "Breaks into your locker to leave little game pieces in there? Doubt it."

I didn't answer.

Zoe turned in her chair and smiled softly. "Sorry. I didn't mean for that to sound harsh. It's probably just some sort of prank or something. Do you know anyone else who got one?"

"Got a chess piece?" I asked. "I dunno. I didn't

have time to ask around."

"That's fine," Zoe said. "I'll ask some of my friends if they've heard of such a thing, but I'd try to keep from saying it was from a secret admirer if I were you. At least for the day."

"The name on the note was 'Jovial Noise,'" I added.

"There was a note with it?" Zoe asked. "And Jovial Noise is who signed it? Doesn't '*jovial*' mean '*happy*?' A *happy* noise?"

"Weird, right?" I said.

"Gavin would probably know more about it," Zoe said with a twinkle in her eye. "I'll find him after class is over and ask!"

My eyebrows rose, and I was just about to say something sarcastic, but lucky for me the bell went off, signaling the end of homeroom. So instead, I smiled. "Saved by the *bell*."

Zoe grabbed her book bag and nearly ran out the door. I dropped the knight back into my bag and zipped it up as my classmates filtered out of the room. Brayden had a seat near the front of the class so he was normally one of the last ones out. As I stood from my desk, I found myself right beside him.

"Hey man," I said.

"Sup?" Brayden replied.

I leaned my head over and shrugged a shoulder. "Not much. Seen any good monster movies lately?"

He shook his head as he stared at the floor.

"Nothing worth mentioning."

I let out a short sigh. "Cool," I said as he walked out the door in front of me. He kept his pace and headed down the hall without glancing back. It was obvious he didn't feel like talking yet so I didn't see any reason to make things more awkward. As he walked away, I murmured under my breath. "Cool."

Monday. 8:25 AM. Art class.

Being the skilled ninja I am, I was able to make it to art only seconds before the bell rang. Zoe was already at her desk getting her painting supplies ready. Brayden was at his spot too, smearing his brush across a sheet of paper.

I walked past Brayden to my desk behind him and took the seat next to my cousin. "So what'd *Gavin* have to say?" I asked her, setting my bag on the floor.

Zoe looked up from her painting. She sighed, leaning her chin against her hand. "He said he was thinking about trying out for the football team…"

Barf. It was gross enough to see my cousin crushing on some dude, but to *hear* her talk about it was even worse. "About the chess piece!" I said sternly.

"Oh," Zoe said with a silly grin. "I forgot to ask."

Brayden turned in his seat to face us. "Chess piece?"

I was surprised that he was talking to me. I stumbled over my words as I pulled the black knight from my book bag. "I uh, yeah, this thing um, was in my locker this morning."

Brayden stared at the game piece. Finally, he said, "I got something like that in my locker too."

"Really?" I asked. "Was it the other knight piece?"

He pushed his hand into his pocket and fished out the chess piece he was talking about. It was different than the one I had. "I didn't get the knight," Brayden said. "I got this little pawn piece."

I was familiar enough with chess to know that the pawns were the little guys in front of the king and queen. They were all the same tiny pieces with the ball on top. "What's it mean?" I asked.

Zoe turned in her chair, interested in the conversation. She looked at Brayden's chess piece. "The pawns are considered the expendable pieces. Y'know, the pieces in the game that are easily given up. I play a lot of chess with my dad so I know a little bit about it."

"Great," Brayden sighed. "I got a lame-o piece while Chase gets the cool horsie. Story of my life, isn't it?"

"It's a knight," I said.

"Whatever," Brayden replied as he tossed his chess piece onto my desk. "Keep it. Whatever it is, I don't care about it."

I didn't want to let the conversation go just yet. "Was this all you got? Was there anything else with it? Maybe... a *note* or something?"

Brayden shook his head. "No, I didn't get a note, but there *was* a thin stick next to it."

"A thin stick?" I asked, confused. "What kind of

thin stick are you talking about?"

Brayden pulled his bag onto his desk and unzipped it. He grabbed the stick he spoke of and set it next to the chess piece. "This was next to the pawn, but I don't know what it is."

Looking at it, I couldn't tell what it was either. "Maybe it's one half of a set of chopsticks," I joked.

Zoe snatched it from Brayden's hand and held it between her thumb and first two fingers, tapping it rapidly on her desk. "It's a conductor's baton!"

I stared at her, trying to understand what her words meant. Clearly my cousin knew exactly what it was, but I still didn't have a clue even after she said it. My confusion must've been obvious.

Rolling her eyes, Zoe said, "It's the little stick that the person leading an orchestra has."

"Someone *leads* an orchestra?" Brayden asked. "Where do they take them?"

My cousin shut her eyes and leaned her head back.

"It's the guy who stands in front of the orchestra and keeps everyone playing in tune with each other."

"Oh!" I said, suddenly understanding. "I know that guy! He like, waves his arms around and dances while everyone plays their violins and cellos and stuff!"

"Exactly," Zoe said, imitating a conductor by creating swooping loops with the baton. "They use this thing when they do it."

"But why would that have been on my desk?" Brayden asked.

Zoe shrugged her shoulders. "I dunno. A pawn piece and a baton? It's a bizarre combination."

I thought for a moment and then remembered the sticky note that was under my knight piece. I started speaking, but stopped immediately. "But I also had –"

Brayden waited for me to finish, but I didn't. The note said "the game was afoot," and I felt it best to keep it to myself, at least until I knew who sent the message.

"Also what?" Brayden asked.

I shook my head, spinning my chair so I faced my desk. "Nothing," I snipped. "I also think, uh… that this whole thing is someone's idea of a lame prank."

I waited for Brayden to say something else, but he never did. I heard him get up from his desk to get more art supplies from the closet across the room. While he was gone, I snuck a peek at his painting. It was of a man in the middle of transforming into a werewolf – of course it would be. This was *Brayden* we're talking about.

The rest of class went smooth and was actually

pretty quiet. It was a workday so everyone kept their heads buried in their own projects. Days like this were cool because the art teacher allowed us to listen to headphones if we brought our own music.

Brayden didn't say anything else about his chess piece. I decided that if he was just gonna ignore me then I shouldn't even bother helping him. Maybe the whole thing was nothing anyway, right?

Yeah, right. If it were *only* that easy.

Monday. 11:45 AM. The end of lunch.

I decided to let this whole chess piece thing roll off my shoulders, and to be honest it felt good. There was a small part of me that wanted to investigate and help Brayden, but there was a bigger part of me that didn't *want* to care.

After scarfing down my lunch, I headed into the school lobby where Mr. Cooper, the gym teacher, was talking to Principal Davis. They both said hello and waved me on my way. For the last month, they've watched me leave the lunchroom and go toward the west end of the school. I'd walk right by them, and they'd let me go because I was the founder of a club that met during lunch.

That's right, I created a club at Buchanan School. We'll have our own picture and everything in the yearbook.

It's so unlike me to have created a club, and a few of you have probably already thought that. I'm sure the rest of you are wondering what *kind* of club I started.

I approached the door to the empty English room and glanced over my shoulder. The sign was already hanging on the doorknob. It was handwritten and said, "Silence please. Martian Language Arts in Session."

That's right. The club I started was Martian Language Arts. Be honest – if you saw a meeting for that, you'd totally skip over it because it sounded like the nerdiest thing on the planet.

But that's exactly the point. The name was so kids *wouldn't* check it out. Why? Because it was the new ninja training grounds.

I pushed open the door and stepped into the classroom. The other members of my ninja clan were already busy training away with each other, but when they saw me, they stopped.

Ever since Buchanan's president had the old ninja hideout destroyed, we had to find a new place to train. One of my ninjas suggested we use an empty classroom during lunch, but it was *my* brilliant idea to make it a club that nobody wanted to join. So for the past month, we've met here in this room. Without a proper place to store our ninja outfits, we all just wore them under our clothes the same way superheroes do.

"Sir!" shouted one of the ninjas.

I held up my hands. "Easy now," I said. "I know I'm a little late to training so I won't be joining today, but

I wanted to ask you guys a question."

The rest of the ninjas stopped and looked at me. A few of them heard the concern in my voice and pulled off their black masks.

I wasn't ready to tell them everything just yet, but I wanted them to keep an eye out for me. "There's trouble brewing in the halls of Buchanan," I said. "I'm not sure yet what it means – it might mean *nothing*, but I'd like for you to report to me if you see *anything* fishy."

"Anything like what?" one of the best girl ninjas, Naomi, asked.

I took a breath. "I don't wanna give details *yet*. Just report *anything* that seems... *off*."

They all agreed to help, which made me happy. The black ninja clan had grown smaller over the last month or so, but the kids that remained with me were devoted and strong. I would choose them over a group of jocks any day.

Monday. 12:05 PM. Science class.

I stayed and chatted with my ninja clan until the end of lunch, which was only about fifteen minutes. I never told them about the chess pieces that Brayden and I received – or the note.

After I dropped my book bag on the floor, I took my seat next to Faith.

She turned her chair toward me. "Whudup?" she asked.

I wanted to tell her about the chess piece, but didn't. "Nothing," I sighed. "You?"

She shook her head and pointed at Mrs. Olsen at the front of the room. "Don't get too comfortable," she said. "We're switching lab partners today."

My heart dropped. "*What?* Are you serious?" I groaned sinking in my seat. The only other person I really knew in science was Zoe, and I had no desire to be *her* lab partner. "Why would she do that?"

Faith smiled. "It's not the end of the world," she said. "It's good for you to get to know other people, right?"

Folding my arms, I pouted like a little baby. "I don't *want* to get to know anyone else."

Zoe walked up behind me. "The seating list is at the front of the class, but it's cool. When I checked my name, I found yours too."

"Great," I said, lifting my book bag once again. "Who am I stuck with now?"

"Olivia," Zoe smirked. She pointed clear across the room at the empty seat next to the girl named Olivia. "She's a sweet girl, Chase. Don't go breakin' hearts now."

I pulled my strap over my shoulder and whispered under my breath. "Whatever."

Weaving between science desks, I finally reached my destination next to a girl I've never spoken to in my life. She wasn't weird or anything, but she *was* one of the quieter students at Buchanan. Who was I to judge her though? I was the same way.

Her hair was black and kind of messy, but a good kind of messy, y'know what I mean? The kind of messy that says "I ride in cars with my window down, so what?"

"Hey, Olivia" I said, cool as a cucumber. "Looks like we're lab partners now."

Olivia glanced up at me from her chair. She smiled. "Call me Olive. I hate the name Olivia."

"Why?" I asked, taking the seat next to her. "It's kind of cool."

"It's an old ladies name," she snipped. "And I'm *not* an old lady."

Boy, two seconds next to her and already things were awkward. I looked back at Faith who was actually sitting *next* to Zoe. Were they lab partners? How was *that* fair?

OLIVE

"Just stay outta my business, and I think we'll get along just fine," Olive said, the smile fading from her face.

Wonderful. Science was gonna be a drag from now on.

After everyone had taken their new places, Mrs. Olsen stood at the front of the room and spoke loudly. "If you all remember, the science fair is after lunch on Friday, so that means we'll be working on our projects in class the entire week."

I shut my eyes and rolled my head back, sighing loudly. "I forgot about that."

"*How* could you forget?" Olive asked. "We worked on our projects all last week."

"I don't mean I forgot about the whole thing," I said, upset. "I mean I just forgot today."

Mrs. Olsen pointed around the room. Lining the counters were the science projects of each sixth grader at Buchanan, even the ones in other sciences classes, which meant there were nearly sixty total projects. "Your stuff is as you left them. When you're ready, you can go ahead and tend to your projects. I'll be at my desk if you need anything."

Olive chuckled. "I saw the volcano you were working on. You know like, twelve other kids are doing a volcano project too, right?"

I nodded. "Yeah, but it doesn't bother me."

"It *should*," she said. "With twelve *other* volcanoes, I bet it's hard to stand out."

The truth was that I wanted to do my project on the history of ninjas and scientifically show how they operated. I'd demonstrate things like creating their weapons, ninja stars, and other stuff, but my parents said no to it. It's probably better that they did though. I'm not sure Mrs. Olsen would've taken it seriously.

"You're right," I said, hoping Olive would just drop

the subject, but she didn't.

"Don't you want to *win* this thing?" she asked. "Don't you at least want to be one of the top three?"

I considered it for a second. "Not really," I finally said. "I just want to get a passing grade."

Olive paused, obviously shocked. "So my lab partner is someone who cares just enough to pass a class... typical *boy*."

That was the second time someone accused me of being too "boy" like. Did they expect me to take it as an insult because it was more of a compliment. I leaned over on the counter with as much swagger as I could muster. "Y'know me," I sighed as I reached for Olive's project to get a better look at it. "Cool as ice without a care in the world."

Olive slapped my hand. "Ah ah ahhhhh," she scolded. "Look, but don't touch."

I was surprised because her project looked like it had been run over by a train. "What's that supposed to be?"

Olive paused. I think I saw tears forming in her eyes, but she looked away too quickly for me to be sure. "It's about the science behind bridges, but... I dropped it over the weekend."

Oh man, this girl was *sad*. I'm still not sure how to handle *sad* girls. After staring wide eyed at the back of Olive's head, I *finally* found the right words to say. "Bummer, dude."

Her shoulders twitched as she peeked back at me.

"Thanks," she said in a low voice.

I slid over and studied the smashed pieces of her project, which now I knew were supposed to be a bridge. "I think it's *fine*. You'll be alright this Friday. Really, I mean look at all the other stuff in here?" I said, pointing my thumb at my own project. "Half of them are *volcanoes*, right?"

I couldn't see her mouth, but the sparkle in her eye told me she was smiling. "Maybe you're right," she said. "I *might* have a chance after all."

"I bet you'll put up a good fight for first place," I said reassuringly. "Winners *win*."

Turning around, she looked at her half broken project and repeated my words. "Winners win…"

Suddenly someone burst through the front door of the science class, banging against the wall so hard it made everyone jump. It was Gavin, the hall monitor captain.

"Mrs. Olsen!" Gavin shouted. "Come quick!"

Mrs. Olsen jumped from her desk and spoke, rapidly walking to the door. "What is it? Is everything alright?"

Gavin shook his head with his eyes peeled wide open. "No ma'am. I'll need you to come with me."

Mrs. Olsen folded her arms and tapped her foot. "What is this, Gavin? Why aren't you telling me what happened? You can't break into my classroom and expect me to just *follow* you."

Gavin caught his breath as he scanned the students

in the class. His stare stopped at Zoe. Tightening his lips, he spoke again. "It's Brayden's science fair project. It's completely destroyed."

The other students gasped. I felt like the air had gotten knocked from my body.

"Destroyed?" Mrs. Olsen asked as she looked at the counters on the sides of the room. "But his project is in here, isn't it?"

Again, Gavin shook his head. "No ma'am. It was found in the orchestra room downstairs. It was *totally* ruined. And it *doesn't* look like it was an accident."

Mrs. Olsen cupped her hand over her mouth. She asked Gavin a few more questions, and followed him out the door. Principal Davis came to take her place for the remainder of science.

I didn't know where Brayden was in the building, but I knew he was probably a wreck. I felt sorry for him as I stared at my own science fair project. Zoe didn't come out and say it, but I knew what she was thinking when we made eye contact. The pawn piece that Brayden was given meant that *his* project was in danger, and the baton might've been a clue that would've led him straight to his project.

This was someone's sick idea of a game. Even the note in my locker said it. The *game* is afoot, and someone wanted us to play with them this morning. To play a game that would cost Brayden a passing grade in science.

My stomach turned sour. Things like that never sat well with me. I knew Brayden wasn't going to be happy, and there wasn't much I could do about it since he hated me. But my throat still tightened at the thought of his destroyed project. I felt guilty for not investigating the chess pieces.

Zoe and I kept our calm for the remainder of school. We agreed the best thing to do would be to find Brayden and talk to him about it, but he wasn't anywhere to be found. He was probably sitting in the front office, trying to make sense of his destroyed science project. Poor guy. He hadn't had the best month.

I decided to do whatever I could to try and make his next day of school better, but it was going to have to wait until the morning.

Tuesday. 7:35 AM. The hallways before homeroom.

Brayden's project had been destroyed close to the end of the school day, but everyone had already heard about it. The project he was working on (a volcano coincidentally) wasn't just broken either. Whoever did it really messed it up. I guess it even looked like they had *fun* doing it. Apparently, it was splashed with black paint before getting smashed apart with a hammer. And all of it was done *in* the orchestra room, which makes me think that Brayden's project was waiting for him to find it before the bad guy killed it.

When I got to school, I walked the hallways looking for Brayden, hoping he would be somewhere in the building. I waited by his locker for a few minutes, but he didn't show up, and kids were already starting to flood the school.

I peeked into the cafeteria to see if maybe he was

eating breakfast, but he wasn't there either. There was only time for one last lap around the corridors, so I gripped my book bag straps and started marching.

Other students were still talking about his project and how it was found. It was weird to hear them gossip about it because I knew I probably could've done something to stop it. Sure, whoever destroyed it was the one to blame, but I was the one who got the knight piece. Part of me felt as if the destroyed project was actually *my* fault.

"Chase!" shouted Faith from down the hall. I couldn't see her, but I'd recognize her voice in any crowd.

I stopped and turned around. "Hey, Faith."

"Pretty crazy about Brayden's project, right?"

I nodded, feeling my throat tighten again. "Yeah, it's awful."

"Have you seen him this morning?" Faith asked.

"No," I replied. "And I even got here early to see if I could catch him before homeroom."

"Right, you two are in the same homeroom, aren't you?"

"Yep," I sighed, searching the crowd of students as we passed them. "I'm pretty sure I won't find him out here."

"Maybe he's in class already," she suggested.

"Maybe," I said. "I've walked by that room a couple times, but he wasn't yet."

Faith lifted her wrist and glanced at her watch. "Oh,

I guess school's about to start in a few minutes. I should probably get to my locker."

I smiled at her. "Me too."

With a playful punch to my shoulder, she spun in place and walked away. I continued down the hall until I got to my locker. There were still a few kids in the corridor so I knew I had a little time left.

After entering my combination, I lifted the metal handle. With a loud thunk, the green door swung open. I stared at the top of my pile of trash, feeling my stomach roll. Sitting on top of the heap was another sticky note, but without the chess piece.

I chewed my lip, staring at the little sheet of paper. I

swear I could hear President James Buchanan laughing in the distance.

I snatched the note and read it quietly. There were only three words written.

"Having fun yet?"

Crushing the paper in my hand, I tossed it back into my locker and slammed the door shut. I didn't bother to get any of my books for the day and headed for homeroom.

Whoever was playing this game was starting to grate on my nerves. When did they get into my locker? *How* did they get in there? Did they have my combination? If they didn't, then they'd need a key, but the only ones who had keys were the teachers and hall monitors. And I'm pretty sure teachers have better things to do with their time than destroy student's science fair projects. And if this *was* a teacher, they'd need some *serious* help. Hall monitors also had keys, but why would they want to terrorize students?

Suddenly I realized that since I received a second note, it probably meant that someone else got another pawn piece.

Zoe had grown pretty close to Gavin, and since he's the hall monitor captain, I figured he should be one of the first people I talked to. I looked at the clock on the wall and saw that I had less than a minute to get to homeroom. The questions would have to wait until after that.

Tuesday. 7:45 AM. Homeroom.

I dropped my bag onto the floor and sat behind Zoe. Everyone else was already in the room and I could hear their conversations of who they thought destroyed Brayden's project. I leaned over to try and get his attention, but his seat was empty.

Mrs. Robinson did her duty as the homeroom teacher, and listed off the announcements like some kind of robot.

I tapped on Zoe's shoulder, but she didn't move. Her attention was fixed on her own book bag sitting on her desk. My aunt (her mom) says Zoe was born overflowing with empathy, which meant she shared the same feelings that others had. I think Brayden was pretty bummed out, which meant Zoe felt bummed *for* Brayden.

But it became clear why Zoe was acting strange. Before I could say anything else to her, she turned and set a black chess piece on my desk. It was the same pawn as Brayden's from the day before. Zoe's project was now in danger.

I was speechless. My jaw dropped as I stared at the chess piece.

"Do you know how hard I've worked on my project?" Zoe asked. "If it gets destroyed, I think I would *explode*."

I couldn't help but smirk at her comment. "But-"
She interrupted me. "*I...*"
"But *this* time-"
"*Would...*"
I folded my arms and waited for her to finish.
"*Explode.*" she finally said.
"But we learned from Brayden's project yesterday," I explained. "This time we know what we need to do."

"Did you get another note in your locker?" Zoe asked.

I nodded. "All it said was, '*having fun yet?*'"

"This kid is some kind of monster," Zoe said. "The kind of kid that probably grew up in detention. You know who this probably is?"

"Wyatt?" I answered.

She nodded.

"But how?" I asked. "He can't get into our lockers without a combination *or* a key, and only the hall monitors have keys."

Zoe's lips melted into a frown. Her eyes glazed over as she stared at the black chess piece on my desk. "Gavin was fired last night. He's no longer the hall monitor captain."

"What?" I asked. "But why? I was gonna ask him about the skeleton key for the lockers!" I sat back in my chair. "I guess I could still ask him. It's not like he loses that information when he's fired."

Zoe looked up at me. I could see fear in her eyes. "That's not the worst part..." she whispered.

I stared, waiting for her to continue.

And then she dropped a bomb of information on me. "Wyatt *replaced* him as the hall monitor captain."

My body lurched forward as I gripped the sides of my desk. "*Are you kidding me?*" I whispered harshly. "How the *spew* does something like *that* happen? Who in their right mind would give him *any* kind of authority?"

"Gavin said it was the president's decision," Zoe

43

whispered.

"*President Buchanan,*" I hissed.

"What?" Zoe asked, confused. "No, the president of Buchanan, you nimrod. I'm talking about *Sebastian.*"

I nodded, swallowing hard. "Right," I said.

Zoe continued. "President Sebastian called Gavin into his office last night and gave him the news. No notice or any reason. Just a 'see ya' and a digital watch as a gift."

"What's the deal with Sebastian?" I asked. "Why hasn't he gotten busted for his candy scandal last month?"

Sebastian was involved in some huge scandal at Buchanan about a month ago that involved candy sales in the basement of the school, which is what kids also called the "dungeon" sometimes. He got busted for it, but was still allowed to be president.

Zoe rolled her eyes. "I don't know," she said. "Maybe nobody really cared about the whole candy thing. Anyway, Sebastian has the authority to hire and fire hall monitors, and last night he exercised that power."

I felt my face grow warm with anger about Wyatt's new position as captain, but I had to push it aside. "So Wyatt has a skeleton key now? That answers the question of who's behind all this."

"That's just it," Zoe said. "Gavin said that Wyatt won't receive a key until later today *after* Gavin turns his in. So it's *not* Wyatt breaking into our lockers."

I folded my hands, shaking my head. "I wouldn't put it past him to still find a way in there. It's *Wyatt*; the kid that's terrorized me since the first week of school, even when he *wasn't* here."

Zoe looked over her shoulder. Mrs. Robinson was still speaking at the front of the room. She was saying something about the science fair at the end of the week, but we weren't listening.

Zoe snatched the pawn back. "This thing means my project is somewhere in the school, and we *have* to find it before it's too late."

"Brayden's locker also had the baton in it," I said. "Was there anything else with yours?"

My cousin reached into her book bag and brought out a stick of women's deodorant. She set the plastic pink container on my desk.

"Sick," I said. "Get that thing away from me!"

Zoe's eyes narrowed. "It's not *mine! This* was the thing next to the pawn in my locker!"

"Oh," I said, relieved. "A stick of women's deodorant? What's *that* supposed to mean?"

"Brayden's project was in the orchestra room," Zoe said. "And he was given a baton. Since I was given this women's deodorant, it could mean that—"

"Your project is in the girl's locker room!" I said, pointing my finger in the air, excited at having figured out the clue.

"Good one," Zoe snipped. "It wasn't exactly the hardest case to crack, was it?"

45

"That's so simple!" I said. "I'll just look around the girl's locker room during gym today!"

Zoe leaned her head with a *very* annoyed look on her face. "Um, here's a better idea – how about *I* check the girl's locker room during gym. I could be wrong, but I don't think *boys* are allowed in there."

"You're probably right," I whispered, nodding.

"Ya think?" she snapped.

"We should definitely tell Gavin about this too."

"I already did when he walked me here this morning. He knows everything – about your chess piece, Brayden's piece, the baton, and the sticky notes. He doesn't know about your new note from this morning, but he probably assumes you got one." My cousin smiled softly. "He's so *smart*."

I rolled my eyes and let Mrs. Robinson's voice flow over me while I thought of my next move. As a ninja, I should be better at catching bad guys, right? So how was it that this person was able to sneak around without getting noticed? It was time to up my game, and with my ninja uniform under my street clothes, switching roles would be a piece of cake.

Tuesday. 10:45 AM. Gym class.

At the beginning of gym, I changed into my gym clothes, but kept my ninja outfit underneath. None of the other kids or Mr. Cooper thought anything of it since it looked like I was just wearing black thermal clothing to keep warm.

I *do* have to say the new jerseys looked pretty slick. Who would've thought a moose for a mascot could look so killer?

After Zoe and I were checked off for attendance, we grabbed a couple of basketballs and tossed them at the hoop closest to the girl's locker room. Several students went outside for some flag football while the rest decided to shoot hoops too. With eight sets of basketball hoops, it wasn't hard to get one to ourselves.

"I can't believe you chose a stupid moose for our mascot," Zoe said.

Maybe I was wrong about how killer it looked? "What do you mean? I think these things look awesome!"

"It looks like the logo for a lamewad nature program," Zoe replied as she tossed her basketball in the air. It landed perfectly in the hoop – nothing but net. I hated how she was such a natural athlete. "Why not a ninja?"

"Seriously?" I asked as I lobbed my basketball toward the hoop. It didn't even go high enough to hit the backboard! "I would *kill* for a ninja as a mascot, but there's no way Principal Davis would've allowed us to be the *Buchanan Ninjas!*"

Zoe caught my basketball after it bounced off the brick wall. "Did you even ask?"

I paused. "No... because I knew he'd say no."

She threw the ball at me like we were playing dodgeball. I squealed, flinching my body, waiting for the impact of the hard ball to hit me, but it never did. I heard her chuckle as she let the ball drop from her hands onto the gym floor. She faked it!

"*Nerd*," Zoe said playfully. If it were anyone else, I would've felt embarrassed, but since it was my cousin, I... *still* felt embarrassed, but laughed it off.

She put her hands on her hips and scanned the gymnasium. "Looks like everyone's distracted well enough," she said. Pointing her finger toward Mr. Cooper's office, she spoke. "And the coach is already leaning back in his chair. We're good to go."

I smirked. "Roger roger."

Zoe leaned against the girl's locker room door. "Just wait here. I didn't see anything the first time I was in here, but I didn't want to make it obvious I was looking. It might take a few minutes though if my project is well hidden."

"What if something happens to you?" I asked, concerned.

"If I'm not back in five minutes," she said. "Just wait *longer*."

And with that, she slipped back into the girl's locker room, disappearing from my sight. This was her mission and she was on her own now. I wanted to go in there and help look because she was my cousin, but there was probably some kind of alarm that went off if a boy set foot in there. I bet the whole room was filled with soft couches and bowls of fruit. I don't know why I thought that – I just did.

"Chase?" asked a girl's voice. "Something wrong?"

I spun around, surprised to see Zoe's friend, Emily, looking rather confused.

When I checked my watch, I saw that two full minutes had passed since Zoe entered the locker room. I must've been standing there with a basketball in my hand, *staring* at the girl's locker room door. If *that* didn't scream "creeper," then I don't know what would've. "Hey, Em, uh… what's up?"

"What are you doing?" Emily asked.

I pointed my thumb at the door. "Zoe's in there. I'm just waiting for her to come out."

Emily's eyes narrowed, obviously suspicious of me. "Alrighty then," she said as she turned back to her friends.

I wiped the sweat off my forehead. That was a *close* one. "C'mon, Zoe," I whispered. "Hurry up before someone else talks to me!"

Of course just as I said that another voice came from behind me. "What're you doing?"

I turned around to see Brayden standing with his arms folded. "Brayden! You missed class all morning! Where have you been?" I asked.

He ignored my question. "*What* are you doing?"

Since he already knew what the pawn piece meant, I didn't think it was a big deal to tell him the truth. "Zoe got a chess piece this morning – the same one *you* got yesterday, but instead of a baton, she got some girl's deodorant. We think it means her project is in the girl's locker room so she's checking it out."

Brayden didn't move a muscle. "So you're helping her get her project back?"

I nodded, excited that maybe my old friend would join the hunt.

He sighed deeply, shaking his head. "Where were you yesterday? When *my* project was being destroyed? You didn't seem to want to find *that* one, did you?"

I stood there shocked, stuttering over my words. Finally I was able to complete a full sentence. "But we didn't know what the whole chess thing meant yesterday! It was *after* we heard about your project that we put it all together!"

"Whatever, dude," Brayden said angrily. "You didn't even try! You probably knew exactly what was happening and let it get destroyed on purpose!"

Was Brayden serious? It *sounded* like a joke, but his eyes looked like they were on fire. "Dude," I said. "I honestly didn't have a clue yesterday…"

My ex-best friend turned around. As he walked away, his voice trailed off. "You don't seem to have a clue about anything ever, do you?"

Clenching my jaw, it took everything I had to keep myself from yelling out. I wasn't angry, but I wanted to defend myself. In a gym full of kids though, yelling out defensively would just look like a scene from a soap opera.

I heard the girl's locker room door creak open as I watched Brayden walk away. Zoe's voice whispered from behind. "Chase! I found it, and it's still in one piece! If you're good to go, I'm gonna take it down to Mrs. Olsen and tell her that someone stole mine too, alright?"

I paused, staring at Brayden as he shot baskets across the room all alone. "Sure," I replied.

The door to the girl's locker room thumped shut. I took a moment, observing the other students in the gym, trying to see if anyone was watching me. Was the kid who stole Zoe's project in here right now? Did they see that we just rescued her stuff from destruction?

I hoped so.

Tuesday. 12:10 PM. Science class.

Zoe returned her project to the science room without a problem. It seemed as if everything was okay. Neither of us got a chess piece or a sticky note since gym so I think it was safe to assume we were good.

After Mrs. Olsen took attendance, she said the rest of class was basically a free day to work on our projects. Everyday for the rest of the week was going to be like that.

I was working on the written part of my project when Faith walked up to me.

"Zoe told me about her project," Faith said.

I set my pencil down. "Yeah," I replied. "I hate to think what would've happened if we didn't find it."

Leaning against the black counter, Faith spoke. "Probably the same thing that happened to Brayden's." With her thumb, she dragged a line in front of her neck and stuck out her tongue, acting like she was dead.

"Probably," I repeated.

"Who do you think it was?" Faith asked.

Olive suddenly appeared out of nowhere and answered Faith's question. "Someone slick enough to move around without being seen."

Faith glanced at me, annoyed.

I looked at Olive. "Who do *you* think it was?"

Olive leaned closer, skimming over the notes to my project. "They never found that *ninja*, right? It's probably *that* kid."

"What?" I asked, surprised. "You think a *ninja's* behind all this?"

"Any kid that wears a mask over his face is bad news," Olive laughed.

Again, I was forced to hold my tongue, but this time it was because I knew the truth. It wasn't a *ninja* that stole Brayden and Zoe's project, or at least it wasn't any of *my* ninjas. "I think it's just the work of someone looking for attention. Someone being a jerk *just* to be a jerk," I said.

Faith chuckled. "It's probably someone that wants to win first place in the science fair, but they know the only way they can do it is to sabotage the hard work of others."

Olive glared at Faith. "It was that stupid ninja from the paper," she sneered. "Just watch. I bet when they catch that kid, the truth will come out! I just hope they catch him before he messes up someone *else's* project!"

My new lab partner stormed away, angered by the conversation we just had, which was messed up because *she* was the one that started it.

"What's her deal?" Faith asked.

I shrugged my shoulders and got back to my own project. "I dunno," I sighed. "Maybe she's just stressed 'cause of the science fair."

Faith smiled softly at me. "You don't have a mean bone in your body, do you?"

"I wish that were true," I said. "I just know what it's like when people talk about me behind my back, that's all."

"How noble," Faith said sincerely as she walked back to her project. "Like a *knight* in ninja armor!"

I thought of the chess piece left in my locker – the black knight. Why would Faith say *that* word? What if *she* was the one leaving the notes in my locker? No. I squeezed my eyes shut and shook my head. Now I was *over thinking* the situation. Faith wouldn't do something like that... would she?

The rest of the school day was cool. Zoe's project remained untouched so we must've won the round. There were still three days left though, and nearly sixty other projects in danger. I wasn't thrilled at the idea of having to do this all over again, but at least my cousin's project was safe.

Wednesday. 7:30 AM. The hallways before homeroom.

When I got to school, I went straight to my locker. I hated the idea that whoever was leaving the notes was able to get in to anyone's locker they wanted, and thought that if I could get there early enough, I'd be able to catch them.

Pulling open my locker door, I saw that I apparently wasn't early enough. Picking up the new sticky note, I read it aloud.

You did well yesterday, but today won't be so easy.
- Jovial Noise

I slammed the door of my locker and rested my head against the cold metal. *Jovial* was really starting to get on my nerves. I wondered how many years of therapy I'd have to go through as an adult because of my *one-*

year at Buchanan School?

Before I left my locker, I set my combination's dial to zero. That way if someone opened it later on, I'd know because the dial *wouldn't* be pointing at zero.

"Hall pass!" shouted a voice.

I turned, groaning at who it was. Wyatt was standing behind me with a bright orange sash draped across his shoulder. There was another larger boy with a red bracelet around his wrist, standing right next to him. Apparently hall monitors were recruiting red ninjas. Wonderful. I was beginning to *hate* this school.

"I don't need a hall pass 'cause school hasn't even *started* yet," I said coldly.

Wyatt grinned stupidly. "Maybe I'll make that a requirement soon, y'know, as my first order of business as the hall monitor *captain*."

I wanted to walk away, but it was still too early in the morning for me to make smart decisions. Resting against my locker, I decided to have a conversation with my worst enemy. "How'd you do it?" I asked. "How'd you get Gavin kicked from the force?"

Surprised that I was talking to him, Wyatt stumbled. "Umm," he hummed, "it wasn't as hard as you'd think. I know people that know people and some of those people even *like* me. Maybe not much, but a *little*."

"I heard *Sebastian* had something to do with it," I said. "Must be nice to be friends with the president of Buchanan."

"Maybe," Wyatt sighed as he pulled a zip locked baggie from the small pocket of his book bag. Inside the baggie were sugar cookies, but *bigger* than the normal kind and bathed in white frosting. For the next few seconds, the only sound was of him opening the seal on his baggie and taking huge chomps out of the cookies.

"I've never seen a cookie that huge," I said, trying my best to sound disgusted. I hoped it wasn't obvious that my mouth was watering for one. They're like my kryptonite!

With a full mouth, Wyatt muttered, "My mom makes them huge like this 'cause she knows how I like 'em. There's enough cookie dough in one of these bad boys to feed a family of six for a *week*."

No way, I thought. I'm from a family of four and there was *no way* a single cookie would feed us for a week! Oh wait… he was being sarcastic.

Crumbs fell from Wyatt's mouth. Wyatt – who was now the hall monitor captain. Wyatt – who was the leader of the red ninja clan that trained somewhere in the school. I stared into his cold eyes and took advantage of his attention by trying to see if he was the one leaving chess pieces around the school. "I *know* it's you, Wyatt."

He stared at me, dumbfounded, as if he wanted to burn me, but had no idea how.

And then I added, "I *know* it was you, *Jovial*."

Wyatt's jaw slowly dropped open. I guess his brain couldn't handle too much thinking at once while keeping his facial expressions normal.

His bodyguard leaned his head over and asked, "What's he talkin' about, boss?"

Wyatt shook his head. "I have no idea," he said to the monitor, and then he spoke to me. "Have you finally snapped? Are you officially crazy? Because honestly that would be *fantastic*."

I grunted, frustrated that Wyatt *wasn't* the science project kidnapper. I quickly changed the subject. "What's your endgame?"

"My what?" he asked. His bodyguard took it as an insult and stepped forward, but Wyatt held his hand up, stopping the larger boy.

"Your *endgame*," I repeated. "How do you see all this ending? You think you can get away with it all?"

Wyatt guffawed like a horse. He glanced over his shoulder and saw some other students approaching so he turned and started walking away. "I've *already* gotten away with it, Chase. You think you can stop my plans, but the *storm* is already coming. You can't stop the weather."

I took a deep breath and held it for five seconds, letting the anger slip away from me. What the *heck* was that psycho kid talking about?

I cinched my bag tighter on my back and started walking among the other students as the hallway bustled with activity. The bell was going to go off at any second, and I had a homeroom to get to.

Wednesday. 7:45 AM. Homeroom.

When I sat at my spot in homeroom, I saw that Brayden was up front already. He was sunken in his chair with his hands folded on his desk. If I had made it to class any sooner, I would've tried talking to him, but as soon as I took my seat, the bell rang.

Zoe immediately flipped around. "Any notes today?" she asked, excited.

I pulled out the yellow slip of paper and held it in front of me. "Yup."

"Have you seen Faith this morning?" Zoe asked as she read the note. "She was looking for you."

My heart skipped a beat. It was nice to hear some *good* news. "Really? What'd she want?"

My cousin made an "I dunno" face by raising her eyebrows and pushing her lips to one side. "She seemed a little anxious." Zoe stopped and glanced at me. "You don't think she got a chess piece, do you?"

I remained silent, feeling my heart skip another beat. Funny how hearts react the same way when they're happy as they do when they're scared. "Man, I hope not. I really *really* hope not."

Mrs. Robinson went on and on with the announcements at the front of the class, but my mind was a haze. Her voice sounded muffled in my head as the world seemed to swirl around me. Everything felt like a bad dream all of a sudden, but a dream I couldn't wake up from. The kind of dream where you're getting chased by a polar bear dressed as a clown – those are the *worst.*

I had to collect my thoughts so I shut my eyes and concentrated, meditating the way ninjas do. When life gets messy, a good way to get it *un*messy is to slow down. At least that's what I've read when studying ninjas. It's as if the world was shouting at me, and I had to make it quiet, even if it was only for a second.

Plus calming myself was a good way for me to think. You should try it sometime – it's relaxing. Just shut your eyes and think of clouds moving slowly against a blue sky. Careful though or you'll fall asleep. Trust me, I know from first hand experience.

"Jovial" was still on the loose. He destroyed Brayden's project; an accident I *would've* prevented if I had understood the game in the beginning. Zoe's project was saved, and apparently still safe. She would've told me if she got another chess piece in her locker, but she didn't so I think the bad guy is going to leave her alone.

Wyatt is the new captain of the hall monitors, but doesn't seem to have any clue about what's going on with the chess pieces. He's a bad egg, but I'll have to hold off on dealing with that until *after* the science fair.

I guess President Sebastian is on "Team Wyatt," but I have no idea why. He defended Wyatt last month when Brayden was busted as a ninja, and then gave Wyatt the position of hall monitor captain, which *also* took it away from Gavin. There's something else going on there, but that too will have to wait.

As for today, I don't know who has the pawn piece. Zoe said Faith wanted to talk, but I *hope* it's not because she received the pawn.

But with my luck... she probably *did*.

Wednesday. 8:20 AM. The hallways after homeroom.

Seconds before the bell clanged, I was already out the door. Sitting in the back of class made it easy for me to slip out a little early. I sprinted through the empty hallway toward Faith's homeroom until there were too many students for me to run anymore. Catching my feet on the carpet, I managed to slow myself down to a casual pace.

I skipped checking her locker since the only period of the day so far was homeroom. Normally kids got their books and stuff for the first part of the day *before* school so there wasn't much of a need to swap anything out until around lunch.

Finally, I saw her at one of the drinking fountains outside the gymnasium doors. I had this thought that I was swooping in to rescue her at the last second until I remembered that I had no idea what was going on with the chess pieces either.

Why was she looking for me earlier? *Please* don't let it be because she had a pawn!

I leaned against the wall while she slurped from the fountain. Trying to act as casual as possible, I spoke, "Sup?"

Faith coughed water out of her mouth, and then smeared her sleeve across the front of her face. "You know I have a *fear* of people freaking me out while I drink from one of these things?"

I felt embarrassed. "Sorry. I just heard from Zoe that you were looking for me this morning."

Without saying another word, she grabbed my elbow and led me to one of the corners of the hallway where the corridor turned. She looked over her shoulder, making sure nobody was following us. With a sigh, she showed me the black pawn piece I *hoped* she wouldn't have.

I felt a sadness melt over my shoulders. "No way," I whispered.

Faith nodded. "It was in my locker this morning."

"No way!" I grunted, punching my fist into the open palm of my other hand. "He's gone too far this time!"

"Zoe told me you helped find her project yesterday," Faith continued. "And that someone left a clue along with her pawn piece."

"He did for Brayden too," I added.

She tightened a smile, but I could tell it was forced.

"You're not gonna like the clue I got."

I remained silent, watching her pull a photo from her pocket. She handed it to me without saying anything.

Studying the photo, I could see that it was a book bag, and that the picture had been taken while the bag was still *on* the person who owned it. The boy in the photo was a little blurry, but I knew who it was immediately.

"This is *Carlyle*," I said. "Why do you have a picture of *Carlyle* and his book bag?"

For those of you joining our program, Carlyle is Wyatt's cousin. He talks like a pirate 24/7, smells like the ocean, and tried to takeover Buchanan School a few months ago. Zoe and I were able to stop him, but since he never broke any rules, he wasn't punished for it. He's a bit of a smooth talker with the ladies, but that's because he keeps his dark side hidden well.

Faith tapped at the picture with her finger. "*That* was the clue I got. This photo was under the chess piece in my locker. What do you think it means?"

I clenched my jaw, feeling my teeth grind against each other. I knew exactly what it meant, and now I knew what Jovial meant when he said today wouldn't be so easy. I sighed, looking at Faith. "It means your project is *inside* Carlyle's bag."

Faith looked flustered. "But my project wouldn't *fit* in his bag," she said, suddenly breathing faster. She was getting panicked. "*What if my project was already destroyed? What if it's in pieces in that pirate's backpack?"* She grabbed my shoulders and shook me. *"Chase, you have to get it back! You have to save it!"*

My brain bounced around in my skull. Taking her hands, I squeezed them tightly. "I'll find a way to get your project back, alright? I promise."

Leading her down the hallway, I tried to think of a plan before the bell rang. It was possible that Carlyle hadn't opened his bag yet since we were just in homeroom so Faith's project might still be in it. I had to get to it before he opened it or else it might lead to an entirely new world of trouble.

Faith squeezed my hand and tugged at me to stop. To my surprise, Carlyle walked right in front of me, even bumping into my shoulder with his own.

"Watch it, mate," Carlyle sneered as he walked through the gym doors.

Finally! I was catching a break! Carlyle having gym meant that his bag was going to be left in the locker room. It even meant that he probably wouldn't open it yet!

I let Faith's hand slip out of my own as I walked backwards toward through the gym doors. I put my finger up to my lips and nodded at her. She knew what I was going to attempt, and she nodded back, half smiling.

"Good luck!" Faith whispered.

"Luck has nothin' to do with it!" I replied. "Meet me at my locker after first period! Hopefully I'll have your project back and in one piece!"

***Wednesday. 8:24 AM. Gym class,
but not MY gym class.***

I waited exactly thirty seconds after Carlyle walked
through the gym doors before I entered it. Keeping my
head down, I went straight for the back of the locker
room, to where the toilets and showers were. *Nobody* at
Buchanan *ever* showered after gym so I knew they'd be
empty. And what's even better is that the lights in the
shower section were switched *off*.

I was in the shadows… the perfect place for a *ninja*.

The bell rang, sounding dull from the locker room.
The guys in the class laughed and joked about pointless
things. Their voices echoed off the shower room walls as
I pulled my ninja hood over my head.

"Hey hold on, you guys," said a boy's voice.

The sound of footsteps pounded on the cement
floor, walking closer and closer to the showers. My body

froze as the boys drew nearer to me. Holding my breath, I forced myself against the wall next to the shower entrance.

The light from the locker room created a perfect rectangle on the tiled flooring. I watched the boy's shadowy figure fill the entrance.

Please walk away. There's nothing in here! Just get to class!

The boy stopped outside the entrance, less than a foot away from me. "I thought I saw somethin' moving in here," he said.

One of his friends answered. "C'mon man, I've seen scary movies that start like this."

"But I swear…" the boy's voice trailed off.

Backed in a corner, a kid is capable of doing some pretty strange things… like attempting a mind control trick. I lifted my fingers slowly and whispered so softly there was hardly a sound. "I must've been seeing things," I said.

The boy put his hand on the open doorway and paused. And then the craziest thing happened. "I must've been seeing things," he said.

It was everything I could do to keep myself from squealing because it worked! Again, I waved my fingers. "Chase Cooper is the coolest."

The boy spoke again. "So that Zoe girl is pretty cute, right?"

Well, that time the mind trick obviously didn't work. And he better stay away from my cousin if he knows what's good for him!

Anyway, I exhaled, relieved to hear the guys walking away. I poked my head out, making sure the coast was clear. There weren't any students left in the locker room, but I saw Mr. Cooper stride toward the exit. He spun in place just as he got to the wooden door, and looked over the room one last time, probably making sure everyone was out. And then he pushed open the door and disappeared.

Instantly, I jumped out of the showers, keeping low to the ground. The long fluorescent light bulbs in the locker room were only at about half power, and by that, I mean most of them were burnt out.

I moved along the shadows as if they were my friends. Like sailing on a river of darkness, I coasted by unguarded book bags that leaned against wooden benches. Carlyle's bag was easy enough to spot since he had an ugly skull and crossbones painted on it.

Suddenly Mr. Cooper pushed opened the door and stepped back into the locker room. I immediately jumped onto one of the benches and launched myself through the air, landing on top of the lockers. It wasn't exactly the quietest thing I've ever done.

Mr. Cooper stopped. "Hello?" he asked loudly.

I straightened my body and kept as still as possible.

"Is there anyone in here?" Mr. Cooper asked as he checked each aisle. "Class is about to start, so you best get out to the gym floor!"

I slowed my breathing as he walked down the aisle right below me. Stopping in front of the lockers I was hiding on, he glanced over his shoulder. I could feel a bead of sweat drip down the bridge of my nose between my eyes. I crinkled my nose, trying to get the bead to stop moving, but instead I made it jump into my eye.

A drop of warm salty sweat right onto my eyeball.

I don't think I have to tell you how much it burned. Let's just say I had to bite my lip to keep from squirming in pain.

Finally, Mr. Cooper turned around and staggered toward one of the desks up front. Grabbing his attendance clipboard, he scanned the room one more time like he was some kind of robot. He shook his head, and disappeared through the exit for a second time.

I smashed my open palm into my eyeball and rolled around. Slipping off the tops of the lockers, I fell hard on the wooden bench and bounced onto the cold cement floor.

In a stroke of good luck, I landed only a few feet away from Carlyle's book bag. I crawled along until it was right in front of me. Part of me felt weird about having to dig through this kid's bag, but the second I lifted it off the ground, I could tell there wasn't anything inside. It was *empty.*

Confused, I rose to my feet with his bag in my hand. I shook it gently, listening for the sound of *anything*, but it never came. I wasn't sure whether Carlyle had forgotten to visit his locker before school or if he was just *didn't* care about school supplies. I grunted, partially impressed. This kid went through the day without his textbooks or pencils? Carlyle really *did* like to live dangerously.

I flipped his bag over, ready to unzip the top of it just to make sure it actually *was* empty, but something on the bottom of it caught my eye. It was another photo, taped to the canvas on the bottom part of the bag.

As I lifted it higher, I saw what looked like a set of numbers from a locker. It was a crusty metal sliver with the digits one, zero, and... *eight.*

Holy oak trees!

Locker 108!

Did your head just explode? Because it felt like

mine did.

It was a picture of *my* locker, lucky number one-o-eight! I even recognized the shape of the nasty crust on the thin metal sliver!

I let Carlyle's bag drop to the ground with the photo still in my hand. As quickly as I could, I threw my street clothes over my ninja outfit and snuck out of the side entrance of the locker room.

First period had only just begun so I had plenty of time to try and figure out what to do before Faith met me back at… *my locker!* She was supposed to meet me back at *my locker* after class!

What was I going to tell her? That Carlyle's bag only had another photo attached to it, and that it was a photo of *my* locker? If Faith's project was inside there, I had to get it out before anyone saw. Brayden's project was destroyed late in the day on Monday, and Zoe's was found completely untouched at the beginning Tuesday. Since it was only Wednesday morning, I hoped it was still safe.

Sprinting through the lobby, I didn't even check to see if there were any teachers or hall monitors walking around. Wyatt was probably somewhere in the halls along with his goons, but I couldn't worry about them at the moment. I just had to get to Faith's project as fast as I could.

I turned the last corner and saw my locker. Slowing to a stop directly in front of it, I rested my hands on my knees, taking a second to catch my breath. I was running so hard that my mouth felt dry, and every breath I took hurt.

I glanced at the combination dial. It was set to the number 24. It *wasn't* at zero like I had left it. During the time between the beginning of school and *before* first period, *someone* had already broken into my locker.

I gulped hard, straightening my posture. I wanted to turn the dial, but I couldn't bring myself to move my hands. I was too afraid of what was inside.

At last, I took a deep breath and reached forward. My hand shook as I twisted the dial, entering my combination. When the last number was set, I gripped the cold handle, but still had trouble finding the nerve to pull up.

"Okay," I said to myself. "This is nothing. Faith's project will be in here and everything will be alright. I'll get it out and take it straight to the science class!"

I pulled up on the handle, hearing the metal click open, but I didn't pull the door out.

"Come on, man!" I said. "You can do this! There's nothing to be afraid of! There might even be another picture clue that tells you to go somewhere else!"

The fear started to wash away as I realized that Faith's project might *not* be in my locker. Buchanan lockers were tall and thin anyways! It was almost impossible to fit an entire science project inside one of these things! I clenched my jaw, and whipped the door wide open.

And then I about puked.

Faith's science fair project was smashed tightly between the metal walls of my locker. It wasn't just *forced* into it either. I looked like someone used their *feet* to cram it into place above my pile of trash.

I started pulling out pieces of her project, hoping it could still be fixed, but the more I removed, the more damage I created. The pink and yellow paint from her crunched up backboard smeared all over my hands and my clothes. It looked like a rainbow barfed all over me! And then, in the blink of an eye, everything got worse.

The fire alarm went off.

I know, right? Just my luck.

My body completely froze up with my fists clenched around smashed pieces of Faith's project. I wanted to run away, but my legs were like, "*Nope!*"

Students poured into the hallway as the fire alarm blasted overhead. I stared at the ground as they huddled around me, shocked. I knew they were saying things, but I couldn't hear them over the sound of the alarm.

Finally, my fists loosened up, and the rest of Faith's project fell to the floor. I gulped again, feeling the chalky paint on my fingers. When I looked over, I saw Faith crying as Zoe stood next to her. My cousin had a disappointed look upon her face.

Brayden came out of nowhere, pushing me against my locker. "Was it *you?* Did you kill my science project?"

I shook my head and shouted frantically. "No! I swear! I was set up!" I looked at Faith. "The clue I found was a picture of my locker! Somebody else did this!"

More and more students filled the hall, staring at me in disgust.

Brayden looked at my hands and shouted over the fire alarm. "If it wasn't you, then why do you have pink paint all over you hands? Why was Faith's project getting strangled by you when we got out here?"

I screamed loudly, trying to defend myself. "*I was trying to get it out of my locker because someone put it in there to make it look like—*" the fire alarm suddenly shut off, allowing me to finish my sentence while screaming at the top of my lungs in the silent hallway, "*I did it!*"

The crowd gasped, only hearing the last three words

of my sentence.

"No wait!" I cried, but it was too late.

Wyatt pushed through the students and stood in front of me. Following behind him was a group of hall monitors, each wearing red wristbands. And behind them was Principal Davis along with several other teachers.

That was it. I was dead meat. I was so dead, they were gonna have to bury me *twice*.

Thursday. 7:45 AM. Detention.

I'd love to say I was able to explain myself and the reason why Faith's science project was in my locker, but I can't. There was too much evidence against me, and Principal Davis was so furious he wouldn't even listen to me. Can you blame him? I had Faith's project all over my hands. If I were him, I wouldn't have listened to me either.

My day ended pretty quickly. I spent the rest of the morning sitting in Principal Davis's office talking with the school psychologist. Of course I told them I didn't do it, but she didn't believe me. Maybe it was because I left out all the details about the chess pieces, and someone singling me out because I was a ninja. I mean, I just wrote that last sentence, and even *I* think it sounds crazy!

My parents were disappointed to say the least. After my dad picked me up, I got a stern talking to. And then when my mom got home from work, I got *another* stern talking to. It felt like the longest night of my life… at least up until I stepped foot into detention the next morning.

"Mr. Cooper," said Mr. Lien, the computer lab teacher who was *also* the detention monitor. "If it isn't the project hater himself."

I shuddered when he said that. Stepping into the ice-cold room, I stared at the empty desks. It was just *me* in detention. I curled lips, faking a smile. "So just sit anywhere?"

The desks all faced the wall and had wooden partitions between them so students couldn't talk to each other. Mr. Lien pointed toward a desk at the back of the room. "You can take that seat back there."

I sighed, dragging my feet across the carpet. The room was so quiet my feet sounded like a monster scraping against a hollow tree. Once I took my seat, Mr. Lien dropped off a stack of papers that were my assignments for the day. He giggled as he patted my shoulder. He was the first teacher I'd seen at Buchanan that seemed to enjoy his job.

Leaning back in my chair, I shut my eyes and stretched my arms out. It was a terrible thing for me to be in detention, but I'm not gonna lie to you – the peace and quiet was pretty nice.

Mr. Lien took his mug from his desk and turned back to me. "Chase, I'll be back in a few minutes," he said, shaking his empty cup at me. "Gotta fill up the ol' coffee barrel. Once homeroom is over, I'll be in and out of here every few minutes. I teach the computer class right across the hall so my attention will be split between both rooms."

"So I'm gonna be completely alone in here?" I asked, hoping it to be true.

Mr. Lien nodded. "Just for short periods of time." He laughed and wagged his finger at me. "Don't you go sneakin' out on me!"

His laugh was frightening, but I did my best to deliver one back. I'm sure it came out as more nervous than I wanted it to though.

Time slowed to a crawl. Whenever I glanced at the clock I was sure it was going to tell me an *hour* had passed, but instead it only said a few *seconds* had! How was that even possible? They say time slows down near heavier bodies of gravity, like black holes, but detention wasn't a black hole... or *was* it?

Was I sitting in the pit of a black hole, sentenced to an eternity of isolation? Did Buchanan School have a secret so deep that even *light* couldn't escape from it? I looked at the door, wondering how much time had passed for the students safe from this wretched room. Was Zoe somewhere in the world forty years older than me now?

I slapped my cheek hard enough that it stung. "OMG, twenty minutes alone in here and I'm already going nuts!"

The bell outside the door started ringing, signaling the end of homeroom. I watched the opening of the black hole as students passed. A sense of fear wash over me at the thought of what detention was going to do to me by the end of the day.

Mr. Lien stepped back into the room and set his coffee cup on the desk. The bell rang out again, starting first period. If I weren't in detention, I'd be in art with Zoe and Brayden. They were probably hard at work on their paintings already.

"Mr. Lien?" said a voice from just outside the door.

I tipped my chair backward to see who it was, but I couldn't.

Mr. Lien walked toward the entrance and spoke. "Yes, that's me," he said. "What can I do for you?"

The kid outside handed over a pink slip of paper. All I could see was their hand.

Mr. Lien took the slip and read it softly, moving his lips. "Ah," he said finally. "I see." Then he stepped backward and gestured for the student to enter. "Take a seat in the back next to Chase."

Gavin, the ex-hall monitor captain entered the detention room. He nodded once when he saw me. Pulling the chair out from the desk next to me, he dropped his book bag and sat down.

Mr. Lien kept his coffee mug close to his face, letting the steam rise around his cheeks and eyes, making him look like an evil dark lord. I hate coffee, but I envied him because the room was so cold. "I'll be right across the hall, boys," he mumbled. "If you need me, feel free to shout from your seat."

Gavin waited until Mr. Lien was in the other classroom before he spoke. Looking at me, he smirked. "Trouble seems to find ya no matter where ya are, don't it?"

I shrugged my shoulders. "I wasn't *lookin'* for it."

"No," Gavin agreed. "But it still managed to creep into your life."

"What's your point?" I asked, frustrated. I didn't need someone else telling me my situation.

"The whole school is up in arms about what happened to you yesterday," Gavin said. "Everyone's already painted you as guilty."

"And what have you painted me as?" I asked, realizing how strange of a question it was.

Curving an eyebrow, Gavin leaned closer and spoke. "Zoe told me 'bout the sticky notes you were getting in your locker from someone named Jovial. She told me 'bout the chess pieces and everything. She also told me you thought the chess pieces meant them kids were in trouble."

"So she basically told you everything?"

Gavin nodded. "Which is why I'm on your side right now."

"Wait," I said. "What're you doing in here to begin with?"

"Wasn't that hard to get in here," Gavin said. "I needed to talk with you *away* from anyone else. In *private.* Figured the best way was to get in a heap of trouble and land myself in detention as well."

I paused. "What'd you do?"

"Let's just say the mice in the science lab got a pretty good view of the cafeteria during breakfast," Gavin said, smiling.

I LOL'd.

Gavin continued. He gestured at me with his open palm. "Look, I get it. I get why you probably didn't give away the fact that the chess pieces were in your locker."

"What makes you think I didn't?"

"Principal Davis would've made a much bigger deal of everything if you did," Gavin said. "The fact that they simply sealed you in here means you didn't rat out the *real* bad guy."

"You're right," I sighed, wondering if it was the right decision in the first place.

"But Zoe and I know you're innocent, even though you were covered in pink and yellow paint yesterday *and* Faith's mangled project was found in your locker."

"I was framed," I whispered harshly, leaning closer to Gavin. "Someone put her project in my locker during homeroom!" I stopped talking, catching myself getting too loud. "How's Faith doing?"

Gavin forced a smile. "She's not as open minded as Zoe and I," he said. "She believes you busted up her stuff. I think she might even hate you."

My heart broke as I sunk into the cold chair.

"I understand," Gavin said. "I'd hate to think of how I'd feel if *Zoe* hated me."

I stared at the floor without saying anything.

"So Mrs. Olsen has everyone's projects on lockdown," Gavin said.

I looked up. "Lockdown? What's that mean?"

"What's it sound like? It means everybody's project is locked away in the room next to Mrs. Olsen's classroom," Gavin said. "It was actually some girl's suggestion. Olivia, I think her name was."

"Olivia is my new lab partner," I said. "She prefers to be called '*Olive*,' like those things I hate on my pizza."

Gavin glanced out the door at the room across the hall. "Olive's the only one with the key to get into the room and she's in charge of guarding the projects. Well, actually it's more of a skeleton key that can get into *any* room in the school, and I think Wyatt and his crew might've gotten a set too. Principal Davis probably has them making rounds close to that room to make sure everything is safe."

I realized I never talked to Gavin about Wyatt taking his position. "What's up with that? Sebastian gave Wyatt your old job?"

Gavin nodded, narrowing his eyes. "Somethin's goin' on there, that's for sure, but I ain't gonna say nothin' until I have proof. Sebastian seems to have Wyatt wrapped around his little finger."

"Or the other way around," I said. "Have you noticed that the rest of the hall monitors have been replaced with members of his red ninja clan?"

Gavin curled his lip, nodding.

"It's like Wyatt used a cheat code to warp to a higher level," I said, proud of video game analogy.

"What?" Gavin asked, confused.

I rolled my eyes. "Nevermind."

"Wyatt's whole thing is a mess in itself," Gavin continued, "but I don't think we should take our eyes off our current situation."

"I agree," I said. "Jovial is still on the loose, and I have no idea who got the chess piece today."

Gavin lowered his eyes and reached into his front pocket. Before he could say anything, I already knew what he was doing. He set a black chess piece on the table in front of me. It was another pawn.

"That's really why I'm here," Gavin whispered. "I need your help."

I stared at the chess piece. For some reason, sitting in the cold room of detention, it seemed more serious than it had before. There was something dark and brooding about the pawn sitting alone at the center of my desk. "Was there anything else with the piece?" I asked, flicking the pawn over. "Everyone else got a clue with theirs."

Nodding, Gavin pulled out a rusted metal combination lock. The dial was caked with dirt. "Just this thing," he said. "Recognize it? It's from—"

"The old ninja hideout," I said, interrupting him.

"Mm hmm," Gavin hummed. "Which means my project is probably around the new bleachers by the track."

"You figured that much out on your own," I said. "What are you doing in here? Why wouldn't you go check the bleachers by yourself?"

Gavin leaned back and propped his feet up on the desk. He had a confident smirk as he put his hands behind his head. "I figured you'd be good at this by now. I thought maybe you'd be able to help with investigating the bleachers."

Nodding slowly, I said. "Fine. I owe you one anyways."

"Owe me?" Gavin asked. "Owe me for what?"

I kicked the bottom of his, causing it to slip out from under him. He landed hard on the carpet, grunting in pain. "For *that*," I laughed.

Standing from the ground, he dusted himself off, which was weird because there wasn't any dust on him. "First we'll have to figure out how to get outta this room."

I looked at the doorway of the detention room. "It's not gonna be hard. I'm not sure Mr. Lien is even paying attention right now. You sure you're alright with sneaking out?"

Gavin's face beamed with a smile. "I'll do ya one better," he said. "I'll get Mr. Lien to *let* us go."

"What?" I asked. "How?"

Gavin tapped his head. "I learned a couple tricks while I was the hall monitor captain."

Gavin stood from his desk and walked toward the door. He turned around and motioned for me to follow.

He peeked his head around the corner to make sure no one was there, and then stepped across the hall to Mr. Lien's computer class.

"Hey, Mr. Lien?" Gavin asked, leaning through the open doorway. I was standing directly behind the ex-hall monitor captain.

Mr. Lien looked up from his desk. "Yes, Gavin? What is it? Is everything alright in there?"

Gavin nodded. "Everything's fine. I was just wondering if it'd be alright if Chase and I picked up some litter around the school."

Picked up litter around the school? Was this kid serious? He was going to get us out of detention by simply *asking* if we could *leave?* And not just *leave* the room, but also if we could *go outside*? I folded my arms, waiting for Mr. Lien to completely reject the idea and scream at us to get back to our seats.

Instead, Mr. Lien waved his hand and looked back at the papers on his desk. "Sure, sure," he mumbled. "Grab those passes on the wall there so nobody stops you. I'll fill out the proper paperwork later, but you'll need to remind me."

My jaw about hit the floor.

"Thanks!" Gavin yelped as he grabbed three plastic passes hanging next to the door. Why would he need three of them? After handing me one of the passes, he started skipping through the empty hallway.

I shook my head in disbelief as I jogged to catch up. "What was *that?* You can just *ask* to go outside and he'll let you?"

"Mr. Lien is on the environmental board," Gavin said. "Whenever his classes have downtime, they go outside and do things to make Buchanan a better place. Sometimes they plant trees and other times they clean up trash. Kids in detention are allowed to help if they know to ask. He considers it community service."

"But what if Principal Davis sees us?" I asked, feeling my heart race at the fact that we had just *walked* out of detention.

Gavin raised his eyebrows. "It was *Davis's* idea! The only thing about it is that kids have to *ask* in order to do it. A lot of students don't know it's an option, and I think they want to keep it private otherwise detention *wouldn't* be detention anymore."

He had a point. If everyone knew they could escape from that black hole, then Buchanan would be overrun with ruffians trying to get a spot in detention. I chuckled at the thought of detention having a wait list. Could you imagine that? Kids fighting over the last open seat in there? How backwards would *that* be?

Gavin passed the lobby of the school, glancing through the tinted glass walls of the cafeteria. All of the tables had a kid or two sitting in them for study hall.

I looked at the clock above the front office. It was 9:10 in the morning. A good half hour had gone by since first period started.

The door to the front office opened, and Mrs. Robinson, my homeroom teacher stepped out. She stopped in the doorway, staring at Gavin, confused.

Gavin lifted his plastic hall pass. "Lien is having us go outside for litter duty."

I forced myself to keep a straight face. Gavin had just said "litter *duty*," but my brain heard "litter *doodie*."

Mrs. Robinson didn't reply. Instead, she smiled and continued down the hall.

The double doors of the gymnasium were just ahead. I sped up until we were walking next to each other. I started to ask what the plan was going to be, but stopped when I noticed we walked right by the gym doors. "Wait a sec – aren't we going out to the track?"

Gavin didn't break his pace. "We are, but not before getting Zoe."

That's what the third pass was for. "Dude, really? Can't we just do this on our own?"

"Zoe's a smart girl," Gavin said. "Besides, she's been by your side this entire time, and right now she knows you're innocent. It would be *good* to get help from her, don't ya think?"

I couldn't argue. Zoe has been nothing but helpful during my entire career at Buchanan. It was just the thought of Gavin and Zoe being an "item" that grated on my nerves. "Fine," I finally said.

Thursday. 9:15 AM. Art class.

I let Gavin do the talking with the art teacher while I waited down the hall. I knew that Brayden would be in class, and if he saw Gavin and Zoe helping me, he'd probably make a fuss about it. It made me sad to know that he was upset with me.

Gavin's voiced echoed off the metal lockers as he spoke with the art teacher. "Zoe needs to come with me to the Principal's office... no, I'm not sure what it's about... yeah, I have her pass right here... okay, I'll have her back to you as soon as possible. Thanks!"

I guess the art teacher wasn't aware of Gavin getting canned from being captain.

Zoe stepped out of the room. As soon as Gavin and her were away from the door, she wrapped her arms around him, giving him a huge hug.

Barf.

When she saw me, she let go of Gavin, embarrassed. "What're you doing out here?" she whispered.

"Gavin needed my help," I replied, folding my arms with gusto, hoping it was obvious that I was grossed out by their PDA.

"I told him to get you," Zoe said. "I knew you'd help. You're too honorable not to."

After saying something like that, how could I be annoyed with my cousin? My face cracked a smile, and I scratched the back of my head. "Well, you know me…"

Zoe turned back to Gavin. "So what's up? What did you guys figure out?"

"Our hunch is that my project is around the new bleachers on the track," Gavin said.

"That's what you think the rusty lock meant?" Zoe asked.

"The lock is from the old lockers in woods before they were torn down," I said. "My ninja clan used those lockers to store our outfits, and like, snacks and stuff."

"Snacks?" Zoe said. "Ninjas have snack time? Do you have nap time too?"

"No!" I snipped. "I mean, yeah, we have snacks, but it's not *snack* time! And only babies have *nap* time!"

"I'm messing with you," Zoe said as she took the lead down the hall. "We'd better get going though. There's no time to waste."

Gavin smiled like a goon, following behind her. I started walking too, but stopped instantly when I heard a familiar voice.

"Hold on there!" said a boy's voice from just around the corner, in front of Zoe and Gavin.

I leaned against the wall knowing full well that it was Wyatt who stopped them. He was like a splinter I couldn't get rid of. And now that he was the hall monitor captain, I feared that it was only going to get worse.

"Hall passes," Wyatt's voice said from around the corner. He had stopped my cousin and Gavin at the spot where the hall turned so he still didn't see me. Another step forward though and I'd be right out in the open.

Gavin lifted his plastic hall pass. "How's the new job going?"

Wyatt chuckled. "Easiest money in the world," he replied.

"You're getting paid?" Gavin asked.

Wyatt paused. "Didn't you?" he asked. "Oh that's right, you *didn't*."

Zoe stepped forward and spoke with a hint of anger in her voice. "If you think you can get away with *any* of this, you're dead wrong!"

I was impressed with my cousin. I knew she had a strong spirit, but I didn't know she was *tough*.

Wyatt took another second before he said anything. He must've been inspecting the hall passes because I saw him hand them back to Gavin. "Everything checks out. Be on your way."

Zoe quickly glanced over her shoulder. I knew she was telling me to hide before she continued around the corner.

I didn't waste any time. As soon as she looked at me, I was gone in the other direction. I knew where Zoe and Gavin were headed. All I had to do was meet them there.

Thursday. 9:30 AM. The track.

It took a few minutes for me to make it to the old ninja hideout. It was so strange looking that I felt like I was having an out of body experience. I saw the spot where the giant log I learned to balance on *used* to be. I felt sad for the days when we used to train in this spot. Is this how adults feel when they see their old stomping grounds taken over by supermarkets? If it is then growing up isn't something I'm looking forward to.

Ducking under the metal bleachers, I waited for Zoe and Gavin to arrive. I decided against slipping on my ninja mask while I was out there. There were just too many students messing around on the field for me to risk it.

Other students in the gym class were playing flag football while the rest kicked a soccer ball around. Mr. Cooper was in his usual reclining lawn chair, sipping on a glass of raspberry lemonade, his signature drink. I'm not sure how focused he was on the class because his head was leaned back, staring at the sky. Wait, was he wearing an *earring?* Has he *always* had that?

"Chase?" a girl's voice asked.

I was beginning to hate the sound of someone using my name as a question. I turned around with that terrible feeling of not knowing what to expect. It was Olive, my new science lab partner.

She leaned her head under the bleachers to see me. "What are you doing out here? You're not in this gym class."

I did my best to stall her while I thought of a good reason for me to be under the bleachers in a gym class I *wasn't* in. My mouth creaked open, and with a hiss, I said, "*Uhhhhhhhhhhhhh.....*"

Olive stared at me, waiting for my answer, but my hiss went on for a good thirty seconds or so.

"Okaaaay," Olive said as she started to walk away.

"How's your project going?" I asked, instantly regretting it because if I would've said nothing then she would've just walked away. Stupid, Chase! Stupid!

"It's coming along," she sighed, leaning her head down again. "I'm not sure I can get it back to a hundred percent, but I might have an ace up my sleeve."

"What's *that* mean?" I asked.

"An ace up my sleeve?" She repeated. "It means I've got a couple days before the science fair. I can figure something out to make it work."

"Why not just start from scratch?" I asked honestly.

She exploded with anger. "Because I've worked on that project for *months!* There isn't *time* to start over and have it be completed by Friday! Do you know how hard it was the find the right pieces to *build* that bridge?"

I shook my head rapidly. "No," I said. "I'm sorry, I didn't mean – I just thought that maybe – I don't know… you're right. Nevermind."

Olive huffed at me and shut her eyes. When she opened them, it looked like the anger had disappeared from her. "Sorry about that. I have a bit of a temper sometimes."

What was wrong with this kid? She had some serious control issues! I bet the amount of *crazy* in her was enough to fill a *lake*.

I waved my hands to let her know it wasn't a big deal. "I get it. Your project is important to you. It's cool."

She smiled softly at me one last time, and then jogged away after saying goodbye. I was going to have to remember to be more sensitive toward her in class.

"Good to see ya made it in one piece," Gavin said as he ducked under the bleachers, but not before allowing Zoe to walk in first.

"Barely," I replied, watching Olive run down the track.

"Huh?" Gavin said.

I shook my head. "It's nothing."

"Did Wyatt see you?" Zoe asked.

"If he did, I probably wouldn't be here," I said

sarcastically.

"Did you see him at all?" Zoe said. "Or the hall monitors that were with him?"

"No," I replied. "I took off before they came around the corner. Why?"

Zoe looked at Gavin, concerned. "They were all wearing those red bracelets," she whispered.

I nodded. "Yesterday morning Wyatt cornered me by my locker, and I saw the same thing. His elephant of a body guard had a red bracelet too."

"It's the red ninjas," Gavin said. "It's like they're seeping into the rest of the school right out in the open."

"Is it a takeover?" I asked.

Scratching his eyebrow, Gavin answered. "If it is, then those guys are doin' it the right way. They've been given *actual* power by becoming hall monitors."

I took a deep breath. "President Sebastian is the one giving them power though. How is *he* in on it?"

Gavin shrugged his shoulders. "I don't know. I've always thought there was something *off* about him, and this just strengthens that idea."

All three of us sat there, staring at each other, unsure of what to say. We knew *something* was happening with the red ninja clan, but didn't know what. There wasn't anything else to say about it so we sat there in awkward silence.

Finally, Zoe looked through the bleachers, watching the other students in class. Then her eyes widened, and she snapped her attention at me. "Is Mr. Cooper wearing an *earring?*"

"*Right?*" I said. "Has he always had it?"

Gavin approached the open slit in the bleachers and looked out at the gym teacher. "I think he's going through some things right now."

"I understand *teenagers* who want to get earrings," Zoe said, "but a forty-year-old man getting one is just *weird.*"

"I hear you guys talkin' about me," Mr. Cooper said without moving in his chair.

I felt my muscles tighten from getting caught. Did he know who it was under the bleachers? Or did he just hear some kids talk about his weirdo earring?

Mr. Cooper continued to stare at the sky. "I lost a bet, alright?"

Zoe's mouth curved into a huge smile as she nodded. Pointing at me, she said, "*There* it is. He lost a bet!"

"Mm hmm," Mr. Cooper hummed. "Now would you mind not staring at me anymore?"

"You got it," I said loudly, ashamed.

Gavin stepped away from the bleachers and spoke. "Can we get back to the reason why we're out here? My science project is somewhere, and I ain't exactly blessed with an abundance of patience!"

Zoe and I stared at Gavin, confused. "What did you just say?" I asked.

"I said let's just find my project and get it back to class!" Gavin said.

I crouched lower, studying the dirt. "Could've just said it like *that*," I whispered.

The new bleachers seemed to stretch for miles around the track. Last month, the school cleared out the entire wooded area to make room for the silver metal eyesore. The trees were ripped up within a day, and the bleachers were put up within two weeks.

Reaching the spot where the old lockers used to be, I scanned the ground for some clues as to where Gavin's project might've been. The earth was hard and dry from the weather being colder this time of year.

"You see anything?" I asked.

Zoe kicked some grass around with her foot. "Nothing yet," she replied. "How about you, Gavin?"

"Nothing," Gavin sighed.

And then I saw it – the corner of a plastic bag

poking out of a pile of leaves about ten feet away. Gavin's name was on a sheet of paper inside the bag. I jogged over to the leaves and started digging through them. Zoe and Gavin joined me, grabbing handfuls of dry leaves and tossing them over their shoulders.

As we uncovered more of the project, it was clear that it wasn't damaged yet. Gavin's papers and pieces to the project were sitting next to each other, carefully placed by Jovial.

"Thank goodness," Gavin sighed when the project was fully removed from the leaves. He wiped a dirty hand across his sweaty forehead.

I was taking a breather, standing behind Gavin and my cousin. "That does it. Your project is safe and sound. I think the day can only get *better* from here."

Zoe turned around to face me. I watched her face go from happy to sad faster than the speed of light as she stared at something behind me. "Think again," she said.

I spun in place, and saw what it was that made my cousin's face white with fear. Under the bleachers behind us stood three members of the red ninja clan wearing their full ninja gear, which included some top-notch armor. The leader's face was covered with a mask, but I could tell from his eyes that it was Wyatt.

"Hall passes!" Wyatt yelled as he jumped at me. I felt a blinding pain on the top of my head, but it suddenly disappeared.

I hopped up from the ground feeling better than ever. Whipping around, I grabbed Zoe and Gavin by their hands and sprinted out of the back of the bleachers. I was moving so fast that it was like I was flying! Then with a whistle, I called a flock of eagles that swooped down from outer space!

"Need a lift?" said one of the eagles with a twinkle in his eye as a lead guitar howled somewhere in the distance.

"Sure do!" I replied.

Zoe, Gavin, and I boarded the Eagle, but it wasn't an eagle anymore – it was a *tyrannosaurus rex!*

I lifted my fist in victory and shouted a battle cry that made the sun explode into millions of drops of light that –

Wait, wait, wait…

I looked down at the dinosaur I was riding, completely baffled. "What's going on?"

"How many fingers am I holding up?" the dinosaur asked.

I stared at the t-rex's tiny little dinosaur hands. "What?"

"I said *how many fingers am I holding up?*"

I opened my eyes and saw a bright white light. The pain on my head suddenly returned when I touched the bump on my noggin. "Am I dead?" I managed to whisper.

"No, but you gave it your best shot," said Gavin's voice.

I rubbed my eyelids, helping my vision adjust. When I opened them again, I saw what looked like the underside of the metal bleachers. I saw my breath as the sound of students playing sports floated in the background. I sat up, looking at the dirt on the ground. "What happened?"

"*Wyatt* happened," Zoe said, hovering over me.

"But I called for the eagles to save us," I mumbled. "What happened to them? Or the tyrannosaur? I thought he was on *our* side."

Gavin looked at Zoe, puzzled. "Maybe he got hit harder than we thought."

Shaking my head, I picked myself off the ground. "No, I was just out of it for a second. Wyatt hit me, and I must've blacked out. Where'd he go?"

Gavin held the pieces of his science project in his arms. "Him and his goons took off after hitting you. I think they freaked out when you didn't get up. They didn't say anything about us finding my project either. It kind of makes me think Wyatt might *not* be the one behind all this."

"Really?" I asked. "He's been on my butt since the beginning of the school year, *and* he just happened to be there yesterday when I was digging Faith's project out of my locker, *and* he's the only one with access to the locked down projects, *and* he just happened to be out here when we were looking for yours? There's a lot of '*ands*' in that sentence for me to think he's *not* behind it!"

"I don't know, it was weird," Zoe added. "Wyatt didn't even look at Gavin's project. He didn't say *anything* about what we were doing. Don't you think if he was the one behind it, he'd at least give a scary speech?"

"Who knows what's going through that kid's head," I asked sarcastically. "He's crazy, and he's *gotta* be the one behind it all."

Gavin tightened his lips. "When are you gonna hit that kid back?"

Zoe answered for me. "*Never*, because he knows better."

"If I hit him back then the game changes," I said. "Right now, he's just a jerk trying to show how much muscle he's got. If I hit him back, then everything I've stood for falls over. I become another kid in sixth grade who got in a fight."

"Is that some kind of ninja thing?" Gavin asked.

"No," I said, shaking my head. "It's just the right thing to do."

105

Zoe and Gavin helped me to my feet. After making sure Gavin had all the pieces to his project, we walked back to the school. There was no sign of Wyatt or the red ninja clan anywhere on the track. Wyatt might've been one of the meanest kids I've ever known, but I had to give him credit for being a sneaky ninja. To appear and disappear so suddenly in the middle of daylight *wasn't* an easy thing to do.

Gavin returned his project to the locked down science room, and explained what happened to Principal Davis and Mrs. Olsen. He stood up for me, telling them I helped get it back, and that it had been stolen while I was *in* detention. They said they *wanted* to believe him, but it was something that would need an investigation since the evidence against me was too strong. I understood since I *did* have Faith's destroyed project in my locker.

But the rest of the day wasn't terrible. Some teachers were still trying to find all the mice Gavin let out in the cafeteria so he was just as stuck as I was. We had assignments delivered to us in detention, but we didn't touch any of them. Instead, we folded a small triangle and played paper football until school let out.

Best Thursday I've had at Buchanan in a long time.

Friday. 7:44 AM. Right before homeroom.

I got to school dreading what I'd find in my locker. All week, I had been delivered little sticky notes, so why would Friday be any different? When I opened my locker, it was exactly how it had been for the last four days – a sticky note resting at the top of my trash heap.

I took it in my hands, read it aloud, and made my way to homeroom.

Friday. 7:46 AM. Homeroom.

"*Checkmate*," I said to my cousin. "That's all that was written on it. No message and no signature. Terrifying right?"

Zoe nodded. She was in her usual place in the seat in front of me. "Jovial is saying you've lost. Checkmate happens when there're no other moves left."

"Duh," I said. "But lost at what? Lost because I was in detention all day yesterday? Who's project do they have today?"

"Hopefully nobodies," Zoe said. "The science fair is this afternoon, so all this madness should end by then."

I leaned back in my chair. "So do we wait it out and hope it blows over?"

"Yes, because all you have to do is last until the end of the day," Zoe said. "Once it's over, what are they gonna steal then?"

I felt a weight lifting off my shoulders. I *wanted* to ignore the whole thing, but I just needed someone to *tell* me it was okay to do so.

Mrs. Robinson stood at the front of the class. "The sixth grade science fair will be held immediately after lunch so all of you will have to report to Mrs. Olsen's room to move your projects from there to the cafeteria."

"Those of us with projects that *weren't* destroyed," Brayden said loudly from the front of the room.

You know how everyone turns to look at you when some other kid in your class has the same name as you? That's what happened after Brayden's comment, but everyone had angry eyes when they looked at me.

Even Mrs. Robinson sounded like she was upset. "Yes, for those who *still* have projects, you'll need to report to Mrs. Olsen's office."

One of the students near the front raised her hand. "What do we do with the chess piece we got in our locker?"

I sat up, jolted by the girl's question. Did she just ask about a chess piece? The feeling of relief vanished as I realized I'd have another project to find.

Another student raised his hand and spoke before he was called on. "I got one too," he said. "What's it mean?"

Mrs. Robinson looked clueless. "I have no idea what you're talking about. How many of you got a chess piece this morning?"

I couldn't believe my eyes. *Every single kid* in the class raised their hand.

Zoe immediately turned around. "Are you sure that note didn't say anything else?" she asked.

"Pretty sure," I said. "Did you get another pawn?"

She shook her head. "Brayden didn't raise his hand either."

"Because you two got yours earlier this week," I said. "Jovial is now after the rest of the sixth graders at this school."

"This game has gotten out of hand," Zoe said. "You've been chasing after these projects all week only to have to worry about *all* of them now? That doesn't make any sense? Why bother with a few of us during the week if they're just gonna mess with *everyone's* stuff now?"

I pondered it for a second, rubbing my chin with my fingers like an old wise man. Finally, after a minute of my cousin waiting for my answer, I said, "I have no idea."

Zoe turned back toward the front of class and

grunted. She folded her arms and slid deeper into her chair. She acts like that sometimes when she's angry.

With only half a day until the science fair, there was no way I'd find everyone's project in time, but I think that was the point. Whoever did this didn't want me to succeed. The game that Jovial was playing just upped its difficulty setting to "hardcore."

Friday. 8:25 AM. Right after homeroom.

As soon as the bell rang, I dashed out the door. There wasn't any time to waste so I didn't wait for Zoe. She was a trooper though so I knew she'd catch up eventually.

Weaving through students, I rushed straight to the room that had the locked down projects. Taking *that* many projects would mean there was *some* kind of clue left behind, right?

As I ran through the hall, I saw kids showing each other the pawns they found in their lockers. Every sixth grader I passed had one in their hands. It was almost impressive that Jovial was able to get his hands on a couple hundred of the same chess piece.

I finally made it to the door next to Mrs. Olsen's science class. I grabbed the metal handle, hoping it was unlocked.

It was.

I pushed open the door, ready to start scanning the room for evidence, but I was shocked to see that everyone's project was still safe inside. Olive was walking down the center aisle.

Stumbling over my words, I spoke. "I thought… what's… is everything alright?"

Olive looked confused. "Of course," she said. "Why *wouldn't* it be?"

I stepped into the room, catching my breath. "Someone said there was a problem down here."

Looking over her shoulder, she shrugged. "Seems pretty normal to me," she said. "What kind of problem were you expecting?"

I scratched the back of my head, totally stumped. "Did you get a chess piece in your locker this morning?"

Olive paused, staring at me. Finally, she answered. "Yes. How'd… how'd you know?"

"Everyone did," I said, pointing my thumb at the door. "Every sixth grader got a chess piece."

"Huh," Olive grunted. "What's it mean?"

"I don't know," I sighed.

Olive stepped toward me, sliding her hand on one of the countertops. "Did you really do it?" she asked with a hint of smile on her mouth.

"Do what?"

"Break Faith's project."

"No!" I replied, upset that anyone would think such a thing. "I'd *never* do that! Someone *framed* me!"

"*Who* would do such a thing?" Olive asked, hopping up and sitting on one of the desks.

I wanted to blame Wyatt for it, but the truth was that I wasn't certain he did it. So instead, I said, "I don't know. Someone who knows too much about me."

Olive's face twitched. "What's *that* mean?"

"Nothing," I replied, walking out the door. I waved my hand as I let the door slide shut. "See ya at the science fair. If something happens here, come find me."

I heard Olive's voice through the thick wood. "Okay! I'll stay in here and make sure nobody else comes in!"

What kind of game was Jovial Noise playing *now?* All the sixth graders got a chess piece, but none of the projects had been touched. All week I'd been searching for the projects in order to save them so if *that* was the game, then I just won... again. I was glad that Olive was staying behind. I doubt Jovial would try something with a witness. Then again, if it *was* Wyatt, I don't think he'd care about witnesses at all.

Friday. 11:32 AM. Lunch.

Before I went to the lunchroom, I thought I'd pay my ninja clan a visit. With all the excitement in the week, I realized I'd only seen them once on Monday. None of them would mind, but I still felt like I let them down.

I entered the training room that had the Martian Language Arts sign hanging from the door. The other members of the clan were already in the room talking with each other. They were all wearing their ninja outfits under their street clothes like me.

"Sir!" they shouted together, standing at attention.

I dragged my feet across the room as I made my way to one of the seats in the back. "It's been a long weeks, guys."

One of the petite ninjas walked toward me. It was Naomi. She fumbled over her words nervously until she finally asked, "Was it *you* that destroyed Faith's project?"

"Of course not," I said, saddened by her question.

She sighed, relieved. "We knew it, but had to hear it from you." She pulled off her black ninja mask and spoke again. "The red ninja clan has grown stronger this week."

"I know," I said with a whiny voice. "Wyatt's taken the position of hall monitor captain, and I think he's replaced all the regular hall monitors with members from the red clan."

Naomi nodded. "We saw that too," she said softly.

"They're planning *something*," I said. "But I have no idea *what*, and with the week I've had, I haven't had time to check into it."

Naomi smiled. "Lucky for you, you lead a loyal clan that'll check into things *for* you when you're too busy."

Then a boy named Cain stepped forward and spoke. "Wyatt *has* replaced the hall monitors with the red ninja clan. It *was* Sebastian that allowed him to do so. We're not sure what their goal is, but we know it has something to do with power. Sebastian doesn't have the cleanest track record as the president of Buchanan. In fact, he almost got kicked from the position last month during a candy scandal."

"I heard about that," I said. "Who helped catch him?"

"Brody," Naomi replied.

"That's right," I said, shaking my finger. "Brody Valentine. Cool last name."

Cain continued. "What we *do* know is that Wyatt

has been hired as Sebastian's personal body guard, which is the reason for him becoming the hall monitor captain. We think that if Sebastian has a team of bad eggs working for him, it'd be easier for him to get away with trouble."

I leaned against the desk, thinking about what my ninja clan was saying. "Is Sebastian related to Wyatt in any way?" I asked. Carlyle ended up being Wyatt's cousin, so I was worried that Sebastian might be too. It would be way too predictable, but I still had to ask.

The petite ninja girl shook her head. "No," she said. "We wondered the same thing. They're not related at all."

"Good," I said. "I don't know what I'd do if there were *three* members of that family at this school."

Cain straightened his posture and folded his arms. "What do you think we should do about Wyatt and Sebastian?"

I rolled my eyes. "Nothing for now," I said. "We have more important things to worry about."

"*More* important than the red ninjas taking over the school?" Cain asked.

I paused. "Did you get a chess piece in your locker this morning?"

All of the members of my clan glanced at each other and then back at me.

"*That's* what's more important today," I said. "That chess piece means your projects are in danger. Everyone who got a pawn this week has had their project stolen. I was able to save Zoe's and Gavin's stuff, but I wasn't fast enough for Faith's."

"Or Brayden's," Naomi added.

"Do you know who it is?" the boy asked?

I shook my head. "I have no clue," I sighed. "It's someone that calls themselves 'Jovial Noise.' Any ideas?"

My ninja clan murmured amongst themselves, but nobody had any answers.

"What kind of parents name their kid 'Jovial?'" Cain asked.

Naomi raised her fist and clenched it in front of her face. "What would you have us do, sir?" she growled.

"I think something big is coming," I replied. "Something bigger than what I've been dealing with all week. *Everyone* got a pawn, so the stakes have been raised by like, a *bajillion*." I walked back to the door and cracked it open an inch. "Keep alert. Hopefully this is all someone's terrible idea of a joke and nothing will happen, but somehow I doubt it."

The ninjas punched their open palms and nodded their heads toward me. I opened the door and slipped into the hallway. The lunchroom was just down the hall and around the corner so I started making my way there. If Jovial was up to something, he'd definitely be in there.

Friday. 11:42 AM. Lunch.

I decided to skip going through the lunch line. I find it hard to eat when I'm stressing about something, and right now, Jovial was the source of that stress. I entered the cafeteria, scanning the seats for *anyone* that looked suspicious.

But in a lunchroom full of sixth graders, *everyone* looked suspicious, especially because they all gave me dirty looks since they still thought *I* was the one who destroyed Faith's project.

The table closest to the door was filled with goth kids, dressed in black and wearing too much eyeliner, even the boys, but I think it's called "guy-liner" for them. A dark and brooding bunch that hunched over their food while they ate, randomly poking a head up to see where a sound came from. It was easy to see Jovial mixed in with those kids.

Jocks sat at the table behind them, but not the typical television jocks you might be familiar with. Sixth grade is still training kids to become full time jocks in high school, so it probably made more sense to call them the athletic kids. A table filled with loud talkers and one-uppers. Jovial might be a good fit for them too since this whole thing might be one huge joke.

The table after the jocks had the cheerleaders. Zoe and Faith were at that table. It was hard for me to think of any of them being the kid I was looking for, but I had to shake that idea from my mind. I didn't *want* to see any of those kids as the suspect.

Most of the rest of the room was filled with your everyday average sixth graders. You know the ones – just trying to get through the school day without making a fool of themselves. Involved in a few extra curricular activities outside of class, such as band or yearbook, but only for something to kill the time before dinner. Not dorky, but not popular either – just invisible kids lost in a sea of other invisible kids. Obviously any one of them could be Jovial.

Beyond those tables, at the edge of the cafeteria, were the true loners. Those who sat by themselves for one reason or another. I know it *sounds* like they'd be losers, but they're definitely *not*. In my time here, I've learned that the most interesting kids are the ones who *don't* follow a crowd. These kids sat alone because they have other things on their mind besides who's going out with who or what kinds of clothes people are wearing. They spend their time doing their own thing – hunting werewolves or starting ninja clans, or dare I say it, talking like pirates 24/7. If there were anyone in the school with enough guts to make a game out of stealing science fair projects, it'd be someone back there.

"Outta the way, jerk!" said a kid.

I looked back and saw that there was a line of students waiting behind me with their science projects in their hands. Mrs. Olsen must've sent them with their stuff to get ready for the fair. "Sorry," I said, allowing the line of students through.

Lunch was nearly over. Kids were tossing their garbage into the bins on the side of the cafeteria. Then they handed their trays to the lunch lady behind the open window of the kitchen.

I saw Faith walking toward me with some of her

friends. Raising my hand, I moved it back and forth giving her a pathetic wave. "Hey," I sighed, nervous.

Faith folded her arms, looked away, and continued walking without saying a word.

Luckily for me, one of her friends spoke *for* her. "She's not into you anymore."

"Not into me?" I asked. "I don't care about that, I just want her to know that I'm sorry, and that it wasn't *me* that broke her project!"

Faith's friend rolled her eyes. "She said you'd say that, and she wants you to know she thinks you're a liar."

I leaned over and looked to see where Faith had walked off to. "Do we really have to do this?" I asked. "I understand she's mad, but the whole 'operator game' is a little *fifth* grade, isn't it?"

"She's mad at you and never wants to speak with you again," Faith's friend said coldly. "It's not even a matter of giving her time because she said when you destroyed her project you basically tore her heart in two."

"That's a little extreme," I sighed, pushing my hands into my pockets.

"Destroying the hard work of others is pretty extreme," the girl snipped.

I waved my arms out as Faith and her friends walked out of the cafeteria. "I didn't do it! I swear!"

Zoe stepped up beside me and grabbed my elbow. "Where's your project?"

Taking a deep breath, I said, "Back in that room Olive was guarding."

"You better get it," Zoe said, pointing at the clock. "Mrs. Olsen said the fair starts right at noon and whoever didn't have their projects up by then would have points deducted."

I nodded, but didn't say anything. I was too frustrated to say anything without sounding mean, and you know what they say – it's better to keep quiet if all you want to do is complain otherwise *you're* the one that ends up sounding like a fool. Well, I'm sure *someone* said that.

Friday. 12:05 PM. The science fair.

It's amazing how quickly the cafeteria can transform from a place where kids eat to a place of scientific presentations. Once all the kids dumped their lunch trash, Mr. Cooper and Principal Davis set up rows of tables for projects to sit on. There was enough room for a student to have their three-piece cardboard backboard and a few extra items on either side of it. Each student had about two feet of space between each other. It was cramped, but every sixth grader's stuff fit.

As I wheeled my project down the aisle, I heard hushed whispers of other students talking about how I broke Faith's project. It took all my strength to stay quiet. Why stay quiet? Because I knew Jovial was somewhere in the room watching me. And arguing with other students about it at this point would be a waste of what little time I had.

I took Zoe's advice and fetched my project from the room next to Mrs. Olsen's, but I made the mistake of thinking I had enough time to choose my spot in the cafeteria. I was one of the last ones to return and saw only a couple spaces left.

Both sides of Wyatt were free, but there was no way I'd be dumb enough to set up there. Brayden had a spot open right next to him even though he didn't have a project, but I decided against that too because I could tell he was still angry with me. I don't know… maybe it was the evil eye he gave me when I looked at him.

Zoe was in the middle of a bunch of her friends so finding a spot next to her was out of the question. Besides, Faith was sitting with her so it was probably for the best.

Every single other spot in the cafeteria was taken. I felt defeated before the fair even began! I decided right there that if I couldn't find another spot, I'd just take the one next to Wyatt. Being next to an enemy is less awkward than being next to an ex-best friend.

"Chase!" shouted a girl.

I turned my head, looking through the crowd of students for the girl that said my name. A few spaces down the aisle, I saw Olive wave at me. I smiled, pushing my cart in her direction.

"I saved you a spot," Olive said, gleefully.

"Thanks," I said, feeling grateful that I didn't have to stand by Wyatt. "Why would you do that though?"

Olive started moving pieces of her bridge project

around as she chuckled. "We're lab partners, right? We should look out for each other now."

That was sweet of her. "Yeah, you're right," I replied.

Staring at her project, Olive spoke again. "Did you figure out what the chess pieces meant?"

With my project on the table, I folded my arms and started scanning the room. "No, not exactly, but I think it means something serious."

"Something serious?" Olive asked. "What *kind* of serious?"

"I don't know!" I said, annoyed. Why was this girl asking so many questions? Why couldn't she mind her own business? From the corner of my eye, I saw Olive staring at me, and suddenly I felt guilty for yelling at her. "Sorry. I'm just kind of freaked out right now."

Olive sat on the table's bench and put her hands on her knees. "Because of the chess pieces..."

I took a seat next to her and leaned back, resting my elbows on my table. "Because of the chess pieces," I repeated. "I just don't have a clue about what to expect."

"Why are you expecting anything at all?" Olive asked softly. "I just don't get it."

I paused, and then decided to fill her in on more details of my week. She saved me a spot so I figured she was cool. "Other students have gotten pawns in their lockers this week too. Those same students had their projects stolen, but they also got a clue that would help them find their stuff!"

Olive stared at me. "So you *didn't* break Faith's project?"

"No!" I said, relieved that someone else finally believed me. "That's what I keep trying to tell everyone, but nobody is listening!"

"Did anyone receive a clue today?" Olive asked, looking at the other projects down the aisle.

"Not that I know of," I replied. "Just the pawn pieces."

"But why do you think it's *your* responsibility to fix all this?" she asked. "Your first few months here weren't the best, right?"

"No, they weren't," I said.

"Then why?" Olive said. "Why bother helping anyone else?"

I didn't even have to think about the answer.

"Because it's the *right* thing to do."

My answer seemed to stop Olive in her tracks. Then she pulled her book bag off the floor and unzipped it. As she fished around the inside, I heard her muffled voice. "So what do you think is going to happen today? I mean, with all the kids receiving pawn pieces and how you got a knight piece, it seems like we're all in for something *big*, doesn't it?"

Wait… did she just say…

I blinked, slowly turning my head toward her. "I never said anything to you about getting a *knight* piece…"

Olive tightened her lips and clenched her jaw. Her muscles twitched in her cheek as her cold eyes glared at me.

I don't think either of us took a breath for several seconds.

Her voice was a soft as a whisper when she finally spoke. "I didn't mean for you to figure me out just yet, but it's happened and now we have to deal with it."

I was floored and didn't know what to do! Could it be Olivia Jones? My new science lab partner was behind the projects being destroyed the entire time? But Olive was so dainty! So petite and soft-spoken! My eyes started to burn from keeping them open too long.

I took a deep *deep* breath to keep myself calm. Glancing over my shoulder to see if any of the other students had witnessed what I had, my brain started connecting the dots.

And then the little light bulb in my head flipped on.

Olivia Jones. Jovial Noise. Both of those names had
all the same letters in them, but they were rearranged to
spell different words. I had been staring at Olive's name
all week without knowing it!

"Why would you call yourself Jovial?" I managed
to whisper.

"Uh, because it sounds *super* awesome," she
replied, grinning. "Villainesses *always* have way cool
names."

She considered herself a villain? Were bullies
villains? I guess it made sense. I mean, Wyatt could be
considered a villain, and he dressed up as a ninja. Carlyle
was a pirate too so yeah, why couldn't Olive call herself
that? Were villains just a different form of bullies? Could
Olive be considered a bully even though she worked

behind the scenes? Was my brain getting twisted thinking about all this? Yes. Yes it was.

"Your game is over," I said as boldly as possible.

Olive chuckled. "Cut the hero voice," she said sarcastically, looking to both sides of her. "The question is what're you gonna do now that you know my secret?"

"If you know me then you'd know I don't fight no matter what," I said. "And there's *no way* I'd ever hit a *girl*."

"Good," Olive replied, bringing her attention back

to me. "I knew you wouldn't, but that's why you're so much fun."

I was confused. "Fun?"

"You don't fight with your fists," Olive said. "You're a very strange ninja."

I felt another chill down my spine from the way she called me out on being a ninja. She obviously knew who I was from the start, but *hearing* her say it made it real. "You've been a tough opponent, but I still don't get it. *What* is this all about?" I asked, hoping she would be a typical villain and reveal her plot.

And she totally did.

"You played along nicely," Olive said. "This entire week I've been playing this game with you, keeping you on your toes with my wild goose chase."

"Wild goose chase?"

"It was like dangling a carrot in front of a rabbit!" Olive sneered. "You just kept on going after the clues I gave you."

"But *why*?"

"You said it best," Olive whispered. "Winners *win*. I broke my project last weekend, you know that. And you also know it wasn't something I could fix so I came up with another plan. I decided that if *I* couldn't win, then *nobody* could."

"By destroying everyone else's projects? But that's cheating!"

"I think it's only considered cheating if I got first place, isn't it? If all I'm doing is making it so that *everybody's* project was ruined, then at least I wouldn't be the *loser.*"

"But why'd you send me on treasure hunts for my friend's projects everyday?" I asked.

"I needed a fall guy," Olive replied. "Someone to pin the thefts on, and I *knew* you couldn't resist a bit of hero work. Brayden and Zoe's projects were to keep you interested in the game. All I had to do was hook you into playing just a little longer until I could stuff Faith's project into your locker, but the fire drill going off while it was all over your hands? That was a coincidence that was absolutely perfect! It was like the stars aligned for me!" She lifted a key in front of her, showing it to me. "All of that was so I could get my hands on *this* thing."

"A key to the room?" I asked.

She nodded, but closed her fist around it and said nothing else.

I felt sick to my stomach. "You're a monster," I whispered. "These kids all worked hard, and you're just gonna take it all away from them?"

"Because it was taken away from me!" Olive hissed. "I'm not gonna get my butt kicked by a bunch of kids who don't give a spew about their science grades!"

"But you did it to yourself!" I said. "*You* dropped your own project last weekend! You kicked *your own* butt!"

Olive folded her arms and stared forward continuing her silent treatment.

I didn't know what to do. I *never* knew what to do

at times like that. "You haven't done anything yet," I said. "Whatever it is you're planning on doing, please don't. Just let the fair go on as normal. Brayden and Faith were the only two whose projects got ruined. I'll take the blame for it, just *please* don't do anything here."

Olive looked at me with her huge doughy eyes. "You'd take the heat for what I've done?"

A smirk cut across my face as I nodded. "If it means the rest of these kids can have a science fair, then yes, I will." I even surprised *myself* when I said that. I kind of sounded like my dad. Maybe I *was* growing up.

Olive held out her open hand. I took at as a sign of surrender, and grabbed it with my own.

"I'm glad to see you –" I started saying, but was rudely interrupted when she pulled me off the bench.

I fell flat on my face on the cold floor of the cafeteria as a few students laughed at me. I watched as Olive dashed away down the aisle. "Sucker!" she screamed.

I flipped up to my feet and started chasing after her. For a small girl, she was *fast*. Tearing down the aisle, I shouted at other students to get out of the way. Most of them did at the last possible second, which made it hard to run at full speed.

Keeping my eyes on the back of Olive's shirt, I jumped onto one of the cafeteria tables. I had no idea where she was going or what her plan was so if I lost her in this chase, I knew she'd get away with whatever she was planning.

Dodging projects on the tabletops, I moved swiftly past the standing cardboard walls that kids set up. By then, I had mastered the art of balance so it wasn't too difficult.

Students shouted at me as I ran through the room. I don't think anyone even noticed Olive as she scampered around them. When she made it to the end of the aisle, she took a hard left turn and started sprinting. I hopped onto the next set of tables and continued following her.

"Don't let him get away!" shouted Wyatt's voice.

I heard screams come from kids as I looked over my shoulder. Wyatt was running at full speed down the center of the table. Everyone in the room was in a panic as he kicked over science projects, running after me.

Great. I'm chasing after a girl *plus* I'm getting chased after. What an awful day this has turned out to be.

I spun around and continued running after Olive, but I suddenly realized I had no idea where she was.

Wyatt's distraction made it so I lost her!

"Wait!" I shouted, turning back toward my enemy.

Wyatt slid to a stop at the middle of the table. I almost thought he was going to tackle me to the ground, but thankfully he didn't.

Catching my breath, I spoke quickly. "The girl I was chasing after is the one who's been destroying projects this week!"

"Liar!" Wyatt yelled.

"No, seriously!" I said. "It was Olive! I was chasing after Olive!"

Faith ran up to the table, and came to my rescue. "I think he's telling the truth! I saw Olive run through here just before Chase did!"

You have no idea how happy it made me to hear Faith defend me. I smiled at her through my heaving breaths.

Wyatt's eye twitched. I could tell something was wrong. "Olive?" Wyatt asked. "Olivia *Jones*?"

"Yeah," I said, suddenly confused by Wyatt's attitude change. "Why?"

"Olive is President Sebastian's niece," Wyatt said flatly.

"What? Sebastian's *niece*?" I asked. "They're both in *sixth grade*, how is that even possible?"

"Sebastian's older sister is like, thirty five years old and married with four kids," Wyatt explained. "Olive is the oldest of the bunch."

"Is everyone at Buchanan related?" I sighed.

"How old are Sebastian's parents then?" Faith asked.

"*Old*," said Wyatt as he scanned the crowd. "Where'd she go?"

The cafeteria full of students turned their heads, looking for the girl who was trying to ruin the science fair. And then suddenly, a figure started running down another aisle toward the stage. Olive must've blended with the crowd when I lost her a few seconds ago.

"There!" Wyatt said, pointing his finger.

But I was already off the table and running after her. Once she hopped up onto the stage, I saw a shiny silver object in her hand, and I realized it was the key. What was she planning on doing with thing? And then I saw a couple of tools at the side of the stage and remembered Mrs. Robinson's announcement from earlier in the week, when she talked about some mild construction due to the upgrading of Buchanan's sprinkler system – a system that had to be *manually* switched on from behind a locked door…

Olive was going to switch on the sprinkler system!

That must've been her plan all along! She needed to get her hands on a skeleton key to open any room at Buchanan, which is why she convinced Mrs. Olsen to lock up the projects. The key was given to her so she could get into the room of locked down science projects, but it conveniently opened any *other* room she wanted too! Olive was a genius!

Olive stomped across the stage to the door at the

back. Fumbling with the key, she slipped it into the lock and pushed the door wide open.

I jumped across the stage and slid like I was going for first base. Just before the door completely shut, I manage to get my foot through. I flipped my ankle, making the door cut open again and rolled into the secret room that had the sprinkler switch.

Once I was inside, I let the door slam shut behind me. I heard Wyatt's body slam into it and then heard him groan in pain. I'm not gonna lie… it made me smile. He was pulling on the handle of the door, but it must've been jammed shut because he couldn't open it. I turned around, thankful that Wyatt was still outside.

The inside of the room was lit by a single yellow light bulb on the wall. It reminded me of a castle from a movie except the walls weren't wet and gross.

I rose to my feet and studied my surroundings, something ninjas do when heading into an unfamiliar area. There were racks of costumes lining the walls along with boxes of hats and feathers and other junk the drama club used for plays – some rope and balls of yarn. The air even smelled musty, as if it had been trapped in this tiny dark room for centuries.

"You're too late," Olive's voice echoed.

I turned, and saw my lab partner standing against the far wall. Her hand was resting on a massive switch that looked like something from one of my dad's old horror movies. Another identical switch was on the other side of her. "Don't do it," I said with my serious voice, but who was I kidding. If she flipped the switch then it was over. The sprinklers would go off and that would be the end of it. Everyone's project would be ruined, and she would get her way.

The smile she had was unsettling. "Give me *one* reason not to, but think carefully on it… because you only have *one* chance."

I inched toward her slowly, racking my brain to come up with something other than "because I said so," but I really couldn't. Finally, I said, "Because you don't want to be remembered as 'that kid who killed the sixth grade science fair,' do you?"

Olive shrugged her petite shoulders and let them slump back down. "Eh," she mumbled. "I've been called worse."

Using both of her hands, she pulled down on the

ancient switch until it clicked. I reached out my hands, but knew I was too far away to stop her.

The metal switch made a wrenching sound of *clack clack clack!*

At that moment, the yellow light bulb switched off in the room, which must have affected the cafeteria too because I heard someone shout, "Who turned off the lights?"

"What?" I heard Olive's voice screech through the darkness. "That's fine because there's only one other switch in the room!"

In the completely dark room, I felt at home. Ninjas *lived* in the dark. It was where we're most comfortable, and where we also had the advantage.

I rolled across the floor, remembering where the costumes and boxes were sitting. Good thing I memorized my surroundings before doing anything else. I grabbed the item I was looking for and slid across the dark floor to where Olive was standing.

"Hey!" her voice shouted. "What're you doing? Let go of my hands!"

I flipped the switch upward, and the yellow light flickered on.

Olivia was sitting on the floor, her hands roped around one of the costume racks. When the lights were out, I managed to grab one of the balls of yarn and spin in around Olive's hands before she could find the sprinkler system switch. And I did it all in a pitch black room.

I'm not one to brag… but that was pretty *ninja* of

me.

I expected to see Olive cry, but she just giggled. "You've beaten me," she said. "You've won *this* round, Chase... best two out of three?"

The door to the room suddenly broke opening, slamming into the wall. Mr. Cooper and Principal Davis jumped through the opening with Wyatt following them like a dog. I saw the faces of other students standing in the cafeteria doing their best to see inside.

Principal Davis rubbed his temples and sighed. "Honestly, Olive, this again? The whole Jovial Noise thing?"

I was shocked. "How'd you know about Jovial Noise?" I asked.

"It's the name she uses when she acts out," the principal answered. "This isn't the first time she's tried something like this, but it *is* the first time she's gotten this far."

I frowned. Zoe was right. If I *had* just gone to the principal to begin with then this whole mess wouldn't even have happened! When I looked through the door, I saw Zoe staring at me with folded arms and a satisfied smile. Then she mouthed the words, "*I told you so.*"

I looked back at Olive, but she wasn't on the floor anymore. Mr. Cooper was already walking her out the door. She stopped just outside the entrance and made eye contact with me. "*Two* out of three," she said with an evil smile before begin escorted to the principal's office.

"Do you have any idea what you've done?"

Principal Davis sighed as he rested his hand on my shoulder.

I looked at him, confused. Was he angry with *me?*

"The new sign came in for the school today," he continued. "A big ol' moose on the front of it."

Oh, he was talking about *that.*

"No matter," he said as he walked toward the exit. "Since you kept Olivia from switching on the sprinklers, I'll let it slide, but maybe we can revisit the idea of a moose for a mascot, eh?"

I laughed, thankful I wasn't in any trouble.

I hesitated before stepping out into the cafeteria. I wasn't sure what any of the other kids were going to say when I did. I really didn't feel like ending the day with any more hatred thrown in my direction.

But when I walked out, everyone cheered. It was crazy. They were so loud that my ears hurt! Shouts of hooray and clapping hands bounced off the walls.

Brayden was the first one to get to me. "So about that whole being *mad* at you thing," he said, staring past me. "Sorry about that."

I smiled at him. "I'm sorry I couldn't save *your* project."

Raising his hands, Brayden patted at the air. "It's not that big of a deal. I think Mrs. Olsen is going to give Faith and I an extra couple weeks to redo ours. We won't get first place or anything, but at least we'll get a passing grade."

I paused. "I really miss hanging out with you," I said honestly.

Brayden shuffled his feet. "Yeah, about that too. Sorry I've been like that. I shouldn't have, I know." Then he smirked at me. "But I think we're even now that you spent the day in detention yesterday."

"Dude," I said, seriously. "Most boring day *ever*."

"I know, right?" Brayden asked. "Like staring into the eye of a black hole for eternity!"

"Yes!" I said, pointing at him. "It's exactly that!"

"Nerd alert!" shouted Zoe over the crowd of loud students.

Faith was next to her. "I'd say sorry too, but I think it's a little sappy so instead..." she trailed off as she punched me in the shoulder. "Good game," she said with a nod.

I rubbed my arm. I knew it was her own way of apologizing. She's cool like that. "No biggie," I said, doing my best to sound like I wasn't in pain.

The crowd of students returned to their projects as I stood on the stage with my friends. I saw boys and girls walking up and down the aisles getting back to their stuff and wondered if they actually knew how close they were to losing all of it.

Wyatt had moved to the back of the room and was keeping watch over each kid that entered or exited. His hall monitor goons were standing guard outside the doors as well.

"We still have them to worry about," Gavin said, stepping onto the stage. "Pretty sure Wyatt's not too thrilled that you saved the day *again*."

"At least it wasn't him I was up against this time," I replied.

"No," Gavin said, shaking his head. "But I bet he makes his move soon."

Brayden stepped forward. "If he does, we'll be ready."

"What about Olive?" I asked. "Did you hear Wyatt say she was Sebastian's niece?"

"So what?" Gavin said. "Who cares?"

I nodded, staring at Wyatt as he waved kids in and out of the cafeteria. His eyes weren't on me, but I knew he was watching me. With a roomful of students, he couldn't say what he wanted to say to me, not like *that's* stopped him before, but as the captain of the hall monitors, he probably needed to watch his step.

"So what's the plan?" Gavin asked.

Zoe, Faith, and Brayden looked at me, waiting for my answer.

"The science fair!" I laughed. "It hasn't even started yet, and we're just doping around on stage!"

I watched as my friends stepped back onto the cafeteria floor. Zoe and Faith joked with each other as they marched back to their projects. Gavin filtered in with another group of students. Brayden stayed by my side.

"Seriously, man," I said. "I'm really sorry I couldn't save your stuff."

"Don't worry about it," Brayden said. "It was a terrible project anyhow."

"You say that, but is there *anything* I can do to make it up to you?" I asked.

Brayden paused. "Horror movies at my place tonight? You bring popcorn, and I'll get the movies?"

I laughed. "Dude, yes! I'll be there!"

We bumped fists, and he jumped off the stage.

I waited another second before returning to my project. I wanted to watch the busy cafeteria just a bit longer. If I had only been seconds slower, this room would be a disaster. Kids and their projects would be soaked in water and tears, but luckily it didn't turn out like that. Maybe the school and President Buchanan *weren't* out to get me after all.

Saved the school from an evil villain named Jovial Noise? Meh, just another typical day in sixth grade.

This whole week had been another nightmare adventure in the weirdest school in the world, but I was calm as I thought about it. I finally felt like I belonged at Buchanan. I was home here, and with friends as cool as mine, I wasn't afraid of anything it might try to throw my way...

...unless it threw *bees*. I'm afraid of *bees* being thrown at me, but... y'know what? Nevermind.

Stories – what an incredible way to open one's mind to a fantastic world of adventure. It's my hope that this story has inspired you in some way, lighting a fire that maybe you didn't know you had. Keep that flame burning no matter what. It represents your sense of adventure and creativity, and that's something nobody can take from you. Thanks for reading! If you enjoyed this book, I ask that you help spread the word by sharing it or leaving an honest review!

- Marcus
m@MarcusEmerson.com

CHECK OUT THESE OTHER CRAZY-AWESOME BOOKS BY MARCUS EMERSON!

Marcus Emerson is the author of several highly imaginative children's books including the 6th Grade Ninja series, Secret Agent 6th Grader, Lunchroom Wars, and the Adventure Club Series. His goal is to create children's books that are engaging, funny, and inspirational for kids of all ages - even the adults who secretly never grew up.

Born and raised in Colorado Springs, Marcus Emerson is currently having the time of his life with his beautiful wife Anna and their three amazing children. He still dreams of becoming an astronaut someday and walking on Mars.

Made in the USA
Middletown, DE
23 March 2015